**He went se‌‍ and‌
lowered his‌ ‍‌‍ ‌l
her.**

Not hot and driven, like before, but slow and
gentle with just enough passion to elicit a
response.

"That is why you're here, *agape mou*," he
murmured as he lifted his head again. "We
are going to kick-start this marriage. *Then*
let us see if you still wish to leave."

Xander could say this in *that* tone of voice
because she'd responded. He could say it
because her fingers were already in contact
with his brown skin. This beautiful, defiant,
contrary creature might not want to want
him—but, hell, she did want him.

Michelle Reid

THE PURCHASED WIFE

HARLEQUIN®

TORONTO • NEW YORK • LONDON
AMSTERDAM • PARIS • SYDNEY • HAMBURG
STOCKHOLM • ATHENS • TOKYO • MILAN • MADRID
PRAGUE • WARSAW • BUDAPEST • AUCKLAND

ISBN 0-373-12470-8

THE PURCHASED WIFE

First North American Publication 2005.

Copyright © 2005 by Michelle Reid.

This edition published by arrangement with Harlequin Books S.A.

® and TM are trademarks of the publisher. Trademarks indicated with
® are registered in the United States Patent and Trademark Office, the
Canadian Trade Marks Office and in other countries.

www.eHarlequin.com

Printed in U.S.A.

CHAPTER ONE

GETTING from flight arrivals to the airport's main exit was like taking a long walk through hell. The whole route was lined with baying reporters, flashing light bulbs and a cacophony of questions aimed to provoke an impulsive response.

Xander kept his mouth clamped tightly shut and ignored provocations like, 'Did you have anything to do with your wife's accident, Mr Pascalis?'—'Did she know about your mistress?'—'Did she run her car off the road to kill herself?'—'Is there a good reason why you withdrew her bodyguard last week?'

With his eyes fixed directly ahead Xander just kept on going, six feet two inches of mean muscle power driving long legs towards the airport exit with no less than three personal-security men grouped around him like protective wolves guarding the king of the pack.

Through it all the questions kept on coming and the camera bulbs flashed, catching his severely handsome dark features locked in an expression of blistering contempt. Inside, his fury was simmering on the point of eruption. He was used to being the centre of media interest, speculation—scandal if they thought they could make it stick. But nothing—nothing they'd said about him before had been as bad or as potentially damaging as this.

He hit the outside and crossed the pavement to the waiting limousine where Rico, his chauffeur, stood with the rear door open at the ready. Dipping into the car, the door shut even before he'd folded his long frame into the seat, while outside his security people dispersed in a prowling circle that kept the reporters back until Rico had safely stashed himself back behind the wheel.

Ten seconds later the car moved away from the kerb and another car was pulling into its place to receive his men.

'How is she?' he lanced, rough toned, at the man sitting beside him.

'Still in surgery,' Luke Morrell replied.

The granite set of Xander's jaw clenched violently on a sudden vision of the beautiful Helen stretched out on an operating table, the object of a surgeon's knife. It was almost as bad as the vision he'd had of her slumped behind the wheel of her twisted wreck of a car with her Titian-bright hair and heart-shaped face smeared with blood.

His jaw unclenched. 'Who is with her at the hospital?'

There was a short hesitation before, 'No one,' Luke Morell answered. 'She refused to allow anyone to stay.'

Turning his dark head, Xander fixed his narrowed gaze on the very wary face of his UK-based personal assistant. 'What the hell happened to Hugo Vance?'

'Nell dismissed him a week ago.'

The simmering silence which followed that tasty piece of information began to burn up the oxygen inside the luxury car. 'And you knew about this?'

Luke Morrell swallowed and nodded. 'Hugo Vance rang to let me know what she'd done.'

'Then why the hell was I not told—?'

'You were busy.'

Busy. Xander's lips snapped together. He was always busy. Busy was a damned bloody way of life! 'Keep something like that from me again and you're out,' he seared at the other man with teeth-gritting intent.

Luke Morrell shifted tensely, wishing to hell that the beautiful Helen had remained locked away behind the gates of their private country estate instead of deciding it was time to venture out and take a look at life.

'It was an accident, Xander. She was driving too fast—'

A pair of wide shoulders shifted inside impeccable dark suiting. 'The point is—*why* was she driving so fast?'

Luke didn't answer. In truth he didn't need to. Xander could put two and two together and come up with four for himself. Yesterday his name had been splashed all over the tabloids alongside a photograph of him standing outside a supposedly discreet New York restaurant with the beautiful Vanessa DeFriess plastered to his front.

His skin contracted against tightly honed face muscles when he thought of the incident. Protecting Nell from embarrassing scenes like that was a duty from which he never shirked. But his bodyguard of the evening had been distracted by a drunk trying to muscle in on them, and by the time the drunk had been hustled away and the frightened Vanessa had been peeled off Xander's front, a convenient reporter had already got his sleaze-grabbing photograph and slunk away.

Nell would have been upset, angry—who the hell knew what went on inside her beautiful head? He'd stopped trying to find out a year ago when she'd married him to a fanfare of 'Romance of the New Century' then promptly refused to share his bed. By the time she'd finished calling him filthy names ranging from *power-driven fiend* to *sex-obsessed moron*, he no longer wanted her anywhere near him.

Liar, jeered a voice inside his head. You just had no defence ready when you were hit with too many ugly truths, so you backed off to hide behind your pride and arrogance.

Photographs of his relationship with Vanessa had been the catalyst then, he remembered. Tasty snippets of truth printed in with the lies that had made it impossible for him to defend himself. He *had* been with Vanessa the week before his marriage. He *had* wined and dined her at a very fashionable restaurant then taken her back to her apartment and gone in with her. The fact that he'd been doing it on the other side of the Atlantic made him stupidly—*naively* believe he was safe.

But back here in the UK, his young, sweetly besotted future bride had been avidly following his every move as it was recorded in the New York gossip columns via the internet.

The sneaky little witch had told nobody. His mouth gave a grim, uncontrolled twitch. She'd come to him down the aisle of the church dressed like an angel in frothy silk tulle and gossamer lace. She'd smiled at him, let him take her cool little hand, let him place his ring on her slender white finger, let him vow to love, honour and protect. She'd even allowed him that one traditional kiss as they became man and wife. She'd smiled for their wedding photographs, smiled throughout the long wedding breakfast that followed and even smiled when he'd taken her in his arms for their traditional bridal dance. If there had ever been a man more ready to be a willing slave to his lovely young bride then, by the time they reached the hotel suite where they were to spend their wedding night, he, Alexander Pascalis, was it.

She'd waited until then to turn on him like a viper. A cold, glassy-eyed English version of a viper, who'd spat words at him like ice picks that awoke this handsome prince up from his arrogant dream-world instead of the prince awakening his sleeping beauty with the kind of loving that should have made her his slave for life.

And sleeping beauty she was then—too innocent to be real. That same innocence had been her only saviour on their miserable wedding night. Still was, did she but know it.

Because his marriage might have turned into a disaster even before he'd got around to consummating it but his desire to possess the beautiful Helen had remained a strong, nagging entity amongst the rubble of the rest.

'I suppose you know why she dismissed Vance?' he queried now, dragging his mind back to the present crisis.

There was a tense shift beside him. Xander turned his dark head again and a warning tingle shot across the back of his neck when he saw the new guarded expression on his employee's face. Luke was wary—very wary. There was even a hint of red beginning to stain his pale English cheeks.

'Spit it out,' he raked at him.

Luke Morrell tugged in a breath. 'Hugo tried to stop her,' he claimed defensively, 'but Nell took offence—'

'Tried to stop her from doing what?'

Luke lifted up a hand in a helpless gesture. 'Listen, Xander,' he said in an advisory voice that sounded too damn soothing for Xander's liking, 'it was nothing serious enough to need to involve you but Hugo was concerned that it might…get out of hand, so he…advised Nell against it and she—'

'Advised her against doing what?' Xander sliced right through all of Luke's uncharacteristic babbling, and by now every bone in his body was tensing up as his instincts shot on full alert. He was not going to like this. He was so damn certain of it that his clenched teeth began to sing.

'A man,' Luke admitted reluctantly. 'A—a friend Nell's been seeing recently…'

Nell felt as if she were floating. It was a really strange feeling, all fluffy and soft yet scary at the same time. And she couldn't open her eyes. She had tried a couple of times but her eyelids felt as if they'd been glued down. Her throat hurt when she swallowed and her mouth was so dry the swallowing action was impossible anyway.

She knew where she was. Had a vague recollection of the car accident and being rushed by ambulance to hospital, but that pretty much was the sum total of her recollection. The last clear thing she remembered was gunning the engine of her little open-top sports car and driving at a pace down the long driveway at Rosemere towards the giant iron gates. She could remember the wild sense of elation she'd felt when the gates had swung open with precision timing to let her shoot right through them without her having to drop her speed. And she could still feel the same sense of bitter triumph with which she'd mocked the gates' efficiency as she'd driven past them. Didn't the stupid gates know they'd just let the trapped bird escape?

Escape. Nell frowned, puzzled as to why the word had jumped into her head. Then she was suddenly groaning when the frown caused a pain to shoot right across the front of her head.

Someone moved not far away. 'Nell…?' a deep, darkly rasping voice said.

Managing to open her eyes the small crack that was all they would allow her, she peered out at the shadowy outline of a man's big, lean, dark-suited bulk standing stiffly at the end of her bed.

Xander, she recognised. Bitterness welled as her heart gave a tight, very painful pinch. What was he doing here? Had corporate earth stopped turning or something? Nothing less would give him the time to visit her sickbed.

Go away, she wanted to say but did not have enough energy, so she closed the slits in her eyes and blocked him out that way instead.

'Nell, can you hear me?'

He sounded unusually gruff. Maybe he had a bad cold or a sore throat or something, she thought hazily. How would she know? She'd barely set eyes on him for months—not since he'd turned up like a bad penny on her birthday and dragged her out to have dinner with him.

The candlelit-table-for-two kind of dinner with good wine and the requisite bottle of champagne standing at the ready on ice. Her fuzzy head threw up a picture of his handsome dark image, the way the candlelight had played with his ebony hair and the golden sheen of his skin as he'd sat there across the table from her with his slumberous dark eyes fixed on her face. Sartorial elegance had oozed from every sleek skin pore. The smooth self-confidence, the indolent grace with which he'd occupied his seat that belied his height and lean muscle power. The lazy indifference with which he'd dismissed the kind of breathless looks he received from every other woman in the room because he was special and he knew he was special, and there was not a person in that restaurant that didn't recognise it. Including Nell, though she was the only one there that refused to let it show.

'Happy birthday,' he said and used long, tanned fingers to push a velvet box across the table towards her. Inside the box was a diamond-encrusted bracelet that must have cost him the absolute earth.

If she was supposed to be impressed, she wasn't. If he'd presented her with the crown jewels she still would not be impressed. Did he think she didn't know that a bracelet like that was the kind of thing a man like him presented to his mistress for services rendered?

Where was his sensitivity? Where it had always been, locked up inside his impossible arrogance, as he proved when he dared to announce then that he wanted to renegotiate their marriage contract as if some stupid trinket was all it would take to make her agree.

She pushed the box back across the table and said no—to both the bracelet and the request. Did it faze him? Not in the slightest. He took a few minutes to think about her cool little refusal then nodded his disgustingly handsome dark head in acceptance, and that was basically that. He'd driven her back to Rosemere then drove away again to go back to his exciting life as a high-profile, globe-trotting Greek tycoon and probably given the bracelet to some other woman—the more apprecia-tive Vanessa, for instance.

'I hate him,' she thought, having no idea that the words had scraped across her dry lips.

The sound of furniture moving set her frowning again, a pale, limp hand lifting weakly to the pain that stabbed at her forehead. Another hand gently caught hold of her fingers to halt their progress.

'Don't touch, Nell. You won't like it,' his husky voice said.

She opened her eyes that small crack again to find Xander had moved from his stiff stance at the bottom of the bed and was now sitting on a chair beside it with his face level with hers. A pair of dark eyes looked steadily back at her from between unfairly long black silk fringes, a hint of strain tugging on the corners of his wide, sensual mouth.

'How do you feel?' he asked.

Pain attacked her from the oddest of places—her heart mainly, broken once and still not recovered.

She closed her eyes, blocking him out again. He shouldn't even be here; he should be in New York, enjoying the lovely Vanessa with the long dark hair and voluptuous figure that could show off heavy diamond trinkets while she clung to someone else's husband like a sex-charged limpet.

'Do you know where you are?' Xander persisted.

Nell quivered as his warm breath fanned her face.

'You are in hospital,' he seemed compelled to inform her. 'You were involved in a car accident. Can you hear me, Helen?'

The *Helen* arrived with the rough edge of impatience. Xander did not like to be ignored. He wasn't used to it. People shot to attention when he asked questions. He was Mr Important, the mighty empire-builder aptly named after Alexander the Great. When he said jump the whole world jumped. He was dynamic, magnetic, sensational to look at—

Her head began to ache. 'Go away,' she slurred out. 'I don't want you here.'

She could almost feel his tension slam into her. The gentle fingers still holding hers gave an involuntary twitch. Then he moved and she heard the sound of silk sliding against silk as he reached up with his other arm and another set of cool fingers gently stroked a stray lock of hair from her cheek.

'You don't mean that, *agape mou*,' he murmured.

I do, Nell thought, and felt tears sting the backs of her eyelids because his light touch evoked old dreams of a gentle giant stroking her all over like that.

But that was all they were—empty old dreams that came back to haunt her occasionally. The real Xander was hard and cold and usually wishing himself elsewhere when he was with her.

How had he got here so quickly anyway? What time was it? What day? She moved restlessly then cried out in an agonised, pathetically weak whimper as real physical pain shot everywhere.

'Don't move, you fool!' The sudden harshness in his voice rasped across her flesh like the serrated edge of a knife—right here—and she pushed a hand up to cover the left side of her ribs as her screaming body tried to curl up in instinctive recoil. The bed tilted beside her, long fingers moving to her narrow shoulders to keep her still.

'Listen to me...' his voice rasped again and she arched in

agony as pain ricocheted around her body. He tossed out a soft curse then a buzzer sounded. 'You must try to remain still,' he lashed down at her. 'You are very badly bruised, and the pain in your side is due to several cracked ribs. You are also suffering from a slight concussion, and internal bleeding meant they had to operate. Nell, you—'

'W-what kind of operation?'

'Your appendix was damaged when you crashed your car; they had to remove it.'

Appendix? Was that all? She groaned in disbelief.

'If you are worrying about a scar then don't,' Xander clipped. 'They used keyhole surgery—barely a knick; you will be as perfect as ever in a few weeks.'

Did he really believe that she cared about some silly scarring? Down in A&E they'd been tossing about all kinds of scenarios from burst spleen to ovaries!

'I hate you so much,' she gasped out then burst into tears, the kind of loud, hot, choking tears that came with pure, agonising delayed shock and brought people running and had Xander letting go of her to shoot to his feet.

After that she lost sight of him when a whole army of care staff crowded in. But she could still hear his voice, cold with incision: 'Can someone explain to me, please, why my wife shares a room with three other sick individuals? Does personal dignity have no meaning here…?'

The next time Nell woke up she was shrouded in darkness other than for a low night lamp burning somewhere up above her head. She could open her eyes without having to force them and she was feeling more comfortable, though she suspected the comfort had been drug-induced.

Moving her head on the pillow in a careful testing motion, she felt no pain attack her brow and allowed herself a sigh of relief. Then she began to take an interest in her surroundings. Something was different, though for the life of her she couldn't say what.

'You were moved this afternoon to a private hospital,' a deep voice informed her.

Turning her head in the other direction, she saw Xander standing in the shadows by the window. Her heart gave a helpless little flutter then clenched.

Private hospital. Private room. 'Why?' she whispered in confusion.

He didn't answer. But then why would he? A man like him did not leave his wife to the efficient care of the National Health Service when he could pay for the same service with added touches of luxury.

As she looked at him standing there in profile, staring out of the window, it didn't take much work for her dulled senses to know his mood was grim. The jacket to his dark suit had gone and he'd loosened the tie around his throat. She could just pick out the warm sheen of his golden skin as it caught the edges of a soft lamplight.

For a moment she thought she saw a glimpse of the man she had fallen in love with a year ago.

The same man she'd seen on the evening she'd walked into her father's study and found Xander there alone. He'd been standing like this by her father's window, grimly contemplating what lay beyond the Georgian glass with its hand-beaten distortions that had a knack of distorting everything that was happening in the world beyond.

That was the night he had asked her to marry him; no fanfare, no romantic preliminaries. Oh, they'd been out to dinner a couple of times, and Xander tended to turn up at the same functions she would be attending and seem to make a beeline for her. People had watched curiously as he monopolised her attention and she blushed a lot because she wasn't used to having such a man show a desire for her company.

Twenty-one years old and fresh back from spending three years high up in the Canadian Rockies with a mother who preferred getting up close and personal with pieces of driftwood she found on the shores of the Kananaskis River than she did with living people. Nell had gone to Canada for her annual two-week visit with the reclusive Kathleen Garrett and stayed to the end when her mother had coolly informed her that she didn't have long to live.

Nell liked to think that her quiet company had given her mother a few extra years of normal living before it all got too much. Certainly they became a bit more like mother and daughter than they'd been throughout Nell's life when previous visits to her mother had made her feel more like an unwanted distant relative.

Coming back to England and to her father's busy social lifestyle had come as a bit of a culture shock. She'd gone to Canada a child who'd spent most of her life being shunted from one boarding-school to another with very little contact with the social side of her industrialist father's busy life. Three years' living quietly with her mother had been no preparation for a girl who'd become a woman without really knowing it until she met Alexander Pascalis.

An accident waiting to happen... Nell frowned as she tried to recall who it was that had said those words to her. Then she remembered and sighed because of course it had been this tall, dark, silent man looking out of the window who'd spoken those words to her. 'A danger to yourself and to anyone near you,' he'd rumbled out as he'd pulled her into his arms and kissed her before sombrely asking her to marry him.

She looked away from his long, still frame, not wanting to go back to those days when she'd loved him so badly she would have crawled barefooted over broken glass if that was what it took to be with him. Those days were long gone, along with her pride, her self-respect and her starry-eyed infatuation.

Her mouth was still dry, the muzzy effects of whatever they'd given her to stem the pain making her limbs feel weighted down with lead. When she tried to lift her hand towards the glass of water she could see on the cupboard beside her, she could barely raise her fingers off the bed.

'I need a drink,' she whispered hoarsely.

He was there in a second, sitting down on the bed and sliding an arm beneath her shoulders to lift her enough to place the glass to her lips. She felt his warmth and his strength as she sipped the water, both alien sensations when she hadn't been held even this close to him since the day of their marriage.

'Thank you,' she breathed as the glass was withdrawn again.

He controlled her gentle slide back onto the pillows then sat back a little but didn't move away. Something was flickering in his dark eyes that she couldn't decipher—but then he was not the kind of man who wanted other people to read his thoughts—too precious, too—

'Your car was a write-off,' he remarked unexpectedly.

Her slender shoulders tensed in sudden wariness. 'W-was it?'

He nodded. His firmly held mouth gave a tense little twitch. 'You had to have been driving very fast to impale it so thoroughly on that tree.'

Nell lowered her eyes on a wince. 'I don't remember.'

'Nothing?' he questioned.

'Only driving through the gates at Rosemere then turning into the lane. After that—nothing,' she lied huskily.

He was silent for a few seconds and she could feel him studying her. Her cheeks began to heat. Lying had never been her forte. But what the devil did not know could not hurt him, she thought with a stab at dry sarcasm that was supposed to make her feel brave but didn't.

'W-what time is it?' She changed the subject.

Xander sprang back to his feet before glancing at the gold watch circling his wrist. 'Two-thirty in the morning.'

Nell lifted her eyes to watch the prowling grace of his long body as he took up his position by the window again.

'I thought you were in New York.'

'I came back—obviously.'

With or without Vanessa? she wondered. 'Well, don't feel like you have to hang around here for my benefit,' she said tightly.

He didn't usually hang around. He strode in and out of her life like a visiting patron, asked all the right polite questions about what she'd been doing since he'd seen her last and sometimes even lingered long enough to drag her out with him to some formal function—just to keep up appearances. He occupied the suite adjoining her bedroom suite but had never slept in it. Appearances, it seemed, only went as far as delivering her to her bedroom door before he turned and strode out of the house again.

'It is expected.'

And that's telling me, Nell thought with another wince. 'Well, I hereby relieve you of your duty,' she threw back, moved restlessly, which hurt, so she made herself go still again. And her eyelids were growing too heavy to hold up any longer. 'Go away, Xander.' Even her voice was beginning to sound slurry. 'You make me nervous, hanging around like this...'

Not so you would notice, Xander thought darkly as he watched the little liar drop into a deep sleep almost before her dismissal of him was complete.

The night-light above her bed was highlighting her sickly pallor along with the swollen cuts and bruises that distorted her beautiful face. She would be shocked if she knew what she looked like.

Hell, the miserable state of her wounded body shocked him.

And her hair was a mess, lying in lank, long copper tangles across the pillow. Oddly, he liked it better when it was left to do its own thing like this. The first time he'd seen her she'd been stepping into her father's house, having just arrived back from taking the dogs for a walk. It had been windy and cold outside and her face was shining, her incredible waist-length hair wild and rippling with life. Green eyes circled by a fascinating ring of turquoise had been alight with laughter because the smallest of the dogs, a golden Labrador puppy determined to get into the house first, had bounded past her, only to land on its rear and start to slither right across the slippery polished floor to come to a halt at his feet.

She'd noticed him then, lifting her eyes up from his black leather shoes on one of those slow, curious journeys he'd learned to recognise as a habit she had that set his libido on heat. By the time she'd reached his face her laughter had died to sweet, blushing shyness.

What a hook, he mocked now, recalling what happened to him every time she'd blushed like that for him—or even just looked at him.

Xander looked away and went back to his grim contemplation of the unremarkable view of the darkness outside the window, not wanting to remember what came after the blushing look.

He should have backed off while he still had a chance then—right off. If he had done they would not be in the mess they were now in. It was not his thing to mix business with pleasure, and the kind of business he'd had going with Julian Garrett had needed a cool, clear head.

Sexual desire was neither cool nor clear-headed. It liked to catch you out when you were not paying attention. He'd had a mistress, a beautiful, warm and passionately sensual woman who knew what he liked and did not expect too much back, so what did he need with a wild-haired, beautiful-eyed *ingénue* with a freakish kind of innocence written into her blushing face?

A sigh ripped from him. Nell was right and he should leave. He should get the hell away from here and begin the unpalatable task of some very urgent damage control, only he had a feeling it was already too late.

The tabloid Press would already be running, churning out their damning accusations cloaked in rumour and suggestion. The only part of it all that he had going for him was the Press did not know what Nell had been in the process of doing when she crashed her car on that quiet country lane.

His pager gave a beep. Turning away from the window, he went to collect his jacket from where he'd tossed it on a chair and dug the pager out of one of the pockets.

Hugo Vance was trying to reach him. His teeth came together with a snap.

And so to discover the truth about his wife's new *friend*, he thought grimly, shrugged on his jacket, sent Nell one final, searing dark glance then quietly let himself out of the room.

CHAPTER TWO

FOR the next few days Nell felt as if she had been placed in purdah. The only people that came to visit her belonged to the medical staff, who seemed to take great pleasure in making her uncomfortable before they made her comfortable again.

The first time they allowed her to take a shower she was shocked by the extent of her bruising. If anyone had told her that with enough applied pressure you could achieve a perfect imprint of a car safety belt across your body she would not have believed them—until she saw it striking across her own slender frame in two ugly, deep bands of dark purple bruising. She had puncture holes and stitches from the keyhole surgery and her cracked ribs hurt like crazy every time she moved. She had bruises on her legs, bruises and scratches on her arms and her face due to ploughing through bushes in an open-top car—before it had slammed into the tree.

And the miserable knowledge that Xander had seen her looking like this did not make her feel any better. It was no wonder he hadn't bothered to come and visit her again.

Her night things had been delivered, toiletries, that kind of thing. And she'd even received a dozen red roses—Xander's way of keeping up appearances, she supposed cynically. He was probably already back in New York by now, playing the big Greek tycoon by day and the great Greek lover by night for the lovely Vanessa.

If she could she'd chuck his stupid roses through the window, but she didn't have the strength. She'd found that she ached progressively more with each new day.

'What do you expect? You've been in a car accident,' a nurse said with a dulcet simplicity when she mentioned it to her. 'Your body took a heck of a battering and you're lucky that your injuries were not more serious. As it is it's going to be weeks before you begin to feel more like your old self again.'

The shower made her feel marginally better though. And the nurse had shampooed her hair for her and taken gentle care as she blow-dried its long, silken length. By the time she'd hobbled out of the bathroom she was ready to take an interest in the outside world again.

A world in which she had some urgent things to deal with, she recalled worriedly. 'I need a phone,' she told the nurse as she inched her aching way across the room via any piece of furniture she could grab hold of to help support her feeble weight. 'Isn't it usual to have one plugged in by the bed?'

The nurse didn't answer, her white-capped head averted as she waited for Nell to slip carefully back into the bed.

It was only then that she began to realise that not only was there no telephone in here, but the room didn't even have a television set. What kind of private hospital was it Xander had dumped her in that it couldn't provide even the most basic luxuries?

She demanded both. When she received neither, she changed tack and begged for a newspaper to read or a couple of magazines. It took another twenty-four hours for it to dawn on her that all forms of contact with the outside world were being deliberately withheld.

She began to fret, worrying as to what could have happened out there that they didn't want her to know about.

Her father? Could something have happened to him? Stunned that she hadn't thought about him before now, she sat up with a thoughtless jerk that locked her into an agonising spasm across her chest.

That was how Xander found her, sitting on the edge of the bed clutching her side and struggling to breathe in short, sharp, painful little gasps.

'What the hell…?' He strode forward.

'Daddy,' she gasped out. 'S-something's happened to him.'

'When?' He frowned. 'I've heard nothing. Here, lie down again...'

His hands took control of her quivering shoulders and carefully eased her back against the high mound of pillows, the frown on his face turning to a scowl when he saw the bruising on her slender legs as he helped ease them carefully back onto the bed.

'You look like a war zone,' he muttered. 'What did you think you were doing, trying to get up without help?'

'Where's my father?' she cut across him anxiously. 'Why haven't I heard from him?'

'But you did.' Xander straightened up, flicking the covers over her in an act she read as contempt. 'He's stuck in Sydney. Did you not receive his flowers and note?'

The only flowers she'd received were the...

Turning her head, Nell looked at the vase of budding red roses and suddenly wished she were dead. 'I thought they were from you,' she whispered unsteadily.

He looked so thoroughly disconcerted by the idea that he would send her flowers that being dead no longer seemed bad enough. Curling away from him as much as she dared without hurting herself, Nell clutched her fingers round the covers and tugged them up to her pale cheek.

'You thought they were from me.' He had to repeat it, she thought as she cringed beneath the sheet. 'And because you thought the flowers were from me you did not even bother to read the note that came with them.'

Striding round the bed, he plucked a tiny card from the middle of the roses then came back to the bed.

'Shame on you, Nell.' The card dropped against the pillow by her face. It was still sealed inside its envelope.

And shame on you too, she thought as she picked it up and broke the seal. Even a man that cannot stand the sight of his wife sends her flowers when she's sick.

Her father's message—brief and to the point as always with him—read: 'Sorry to hear about your accident. Couldn't get back to see you. Take care of yourself. Get well soon. Love Pops.'

Saying not a word, she slid the little card back into its envelope then pushed it beneath her pillow, but telling tears were welling in her eyes.

'He wanted to come back,' Xander dropped into the ensuing thick silence. 'But he is locked in some important negotiations with the Australian government and I...assured him that you would understand if he remained where he was.'

So he'd stayed. That was her father. Loving in many ways but single-minded in most. Money was what really mattered, the great, grinding juggernaut of corporate business. It was no wonder her mother had left him to go back to her native Canada. When she was little, Nell had used to wonder if he even noticed that she'd gone. She was a teenager before she'd found out that her mother had begun an affair with a childhood sweetheart and had returned to Canada to be with him.

Like mother like daughter, she mused hollowly. They had a penchant for picking out the wrong men. The duration of her mother's affair had been shorter than her marriage had been, which said so much about leaving her five-year-old daughter behind for what was supposed to have been the real love of her life.

'You've washed your hair...'

'I want a telephone,' she demanded.

'And the bruises on your face are beginning to fade...' He spoke right over her as if she hadn't spoken at all. 'You look much better, Nell.'

What did he care? 'I want a telephone,' she repeated. 'And you left me with no money. I can't find my purse or my clothes or my mobile telephone.'

'You don't need them while you're lying there.'

She turned her head to flash him a bitter look. He was standing by the bed, big and lean, taking up more space than he deserved. All six feet two inches of him honed to perfection like a piece of art. His suit was grey today, she noticed. A smooth-as-silk gunmetal grey that did not dare to show a single crease, like his white shirt and his silk-black hair and his—

'They won't let me have a newspaper or a magazine.' She cut that line of thinking off before it went any further. 'I have no TV and no telephone.' She gave a full list of her grievances. 'If it isn't my father, then what is it that you are trying to hide from me, Xander?' she demanded, knowing now that her isolation had to be down to him. Xander was the only person with enough weight to throw about. In fact she was amazed that it hadn't occurred to her to blame him before now.

He made no answer, just stood there looking down at her through unfathomable dark eyes set in his hard, handsome face—then he turned and strode out of the room without even saying goodbye!

Nell stared after him with her eyes shot through with pained dismay. Had their disastrous marriage come down to the point where he couldn't even be bothered to apply those strictly polite manners he usually used to such devastating effect?

It hurt—which was stupid, but it did and in places that had nothing whatsoever to do with her injuries. Five days without so much as a word from him then he strode in there looking every inch the handsome, dynamic power force he was, looked at her as if he couldn't stand the sight of her then walked out again.

She wouldn't cry, she told the sting at the backs of her eyes. Too fed up and too weak to do more than bite hard on her bottom lip to stop it from quivering, she stared at the roses sent by that other man in her life who strode in and out of it at his own arrogant behest.

She hated Alexander Pascalis. He'd broken her heart and she should have left him when she'd had the chance, driven off into the sunset without stopping to look back and think about what she was leaving behind, then she would not be lying here feeling so bruised and broken—and that was on the inside! If he'd cared anything for her at all he should not have married her. He should have stuck to his—

The door swung open and Xander strode back in again,

catching her lying on her side staring at the roses through a glaze of tears.

'If you miss him that much I will bring him home,' he announced curtly.

'Don't put yourself out,' she responded with acid bite. 'What brought you back here so quickly?'

He didn't seem to understand the question, a frown darkening his smooth brow as he moved across the room to collect a chair, which he placed by the bed at an angle so that when he sat himself down on it he was looking her directly in the face.

Nell stirred restlessly, not liking the way he'd done it, or the new look of hard intensity he was treating her to. She stared back warily, waiting to hear whatever it was he was going to hit her with. He was leaning back with his long legs stretched out in front of him and his jacket flipped open in one of those casually elegant attitudes this man pulled off with such panache. His shirt was startlingly white—he liked to wear white shirts, cool, crisp things that accentuated the width of his powerful chest and long, tightly muscled torso. Black handmade shoes, grey silk trousers, bright white shirt and a dark blue silk tie. His cleanly shaved chin had a cleft that warned all of his tough inner strength—like the well-shaped mouth that could do cynicism and sensuality at the same time and to such devastating effect. Then there was the nose that had a tendency to flare at the nostrils when he was angry. It wasn't flaring now, but the black eyes were glinting with something not very nice, she saw.

And his eyes weren't really all black, but a dark, dark brown colour, deeply set beneath thick black eyebrows and between long, dense, curling lashes that helped to shade the brown iris black.

Xander was Greek in everything he thought and did but he got his elegant carriage from his beautiful Italian mother. And Gabriela Pascalis could slay anyone with a look, just as her son could. She'd done it to Nell the first time they'd met and Gabriela had not tried to hide her shock. 'What is Alexander playing at, wanting to marry a child? They will crucify you the moment he attempts to slot you into his sophisticated lifestyle.'

'He loves me.' She'd tried to stand up for herself.

'Alexander does not do love, *cara*,' his mother had drily mocked that. 'In case you have not realised it as yet, he was hewn from rock chipped off Mount Olympus.' She had actually meant it too. 'No, this is more likely to be a business transaction,' her future mother-in-law had decided without a single second's thought to how a statement like that would make Nell feel. 'I will have to find out what kind of business deal. Leave it to me, child. There is still time to save you from this...'

'Finished checking me out?' The mocking lilt to his voice brought her eyes back into focus on his face. She wished she knew what he was thinking behind that cool, smooth, sardonic mask. 'I am still the same person you married, believe me.'

Oh, she believed. Nothing had changed. His mother had been right but Nell hadn't listened. Not until Vanessa DeFriess had entered the frame.

'Want do you want?' She didn't even attempt to sound pleasant.

He moved—not much but enough for Nell to be aware by the way her senses tightened on alert to remind her that Xander was a dangerously unpredictable beast. He might appear relaxed, but she had an itchy suspicion that he was no such thing.

'We need to talk about your accident,' he told her levelly. 'The police have some questions.'

Nell dropped her eyes, concentrating her attention on her fingers where they scratched absently at the white sheet. 'I told you, I don't remember anything.'

'Tell me what you do remember.'

'We've been through this once.' Her eyebrows snapped together. 'I don't see the use in going through it a—'

'You would rather I allow the police to come here so that you can repeat it all to them?'

No, she wouldn't. 'What's to repeat?' Flicking him a guarded look, she looked quickly away again. 'I remember driving down the driveway and through the gates then turning into the lane—'

'Left or right?'

'I don't remember—'

'Well, it might help if you said where it was you were going.'

'I don't remember that either.'

'Try,' he said.

'What for?' she flipped back. 'What does it matter now where I was going? I obviously didn't get there.'

'True.' He grimaced. 'Instead of arriving—wherever it was—you left the road at speed on a notorious bend we all treat with respect. You then proceeded to plough through a row of bushes and concluded the journey by piling head-on into a tree.'

'Thanks for filling in the gaps,' she derided.

'The car boot sprang open on impact,' he continued, unmoved by her tone. 'Your possessions were strewn everywhere. Sweaters, skirts, dresses, underwear...'

'Charity!' she declared with a sudden burst of memory. 'I remember now, I was taking some of my old things to the charity shop in the village.'

'Charity,' Xander repeated in a voice as thin as silk. 'Well, that explains the need to drive like a maniac. Now explain to me why you dismissed Hugo Vance...'

Nell froze where she lay curled on her side, her moment of triumph at her own quick thinking fizzling out at the introduction of her ex-bodyguard's name. She moved, ignoring the creases of pain in her ribs to drag herself into a sitting position so she could grab her knees in a loose but very defensive hug, her hair slithering across her slender shoulders to float all around her in a river of rippling Titian silk.

'I don't need a bodyguard,' she muttered.

'I have three,' Xander replied. 'What does that tell you about what you need?'

'I'm not you.' She sent him an acrid look. 'I don't stride

around the world, playing God and throwing my weight around—'

His eyes gave a sudden glint. 'So that is how you see me—as a god that throws his weight around?' The silken tone gave her no clue as to what was about to come next. 'Well, my beautiful Helen,' he drawled in a thoroughly lazy attitude, 'just watch this space—'

In a single snaking move he was off the chair and leaning over her. The next second and he was gathering her hair up and away from her face. A controlled tug sent her head back. A stifled gasp brought her startled eyes flicking up to clash with his.

What she saw glowing there set her trembling. 'You're hurting—'

'No, I'm not,' he denied through gritted teeth. 'But I am teetering, *cara mia*, so watch out how many more lies you wish to spout at me!'

'I'm not lying!'

'No?' With some more of that controlled strength he wound her hair around his fingers, urging her head back an extra vulnerable inch so as to expose the long, creamy length of her slender throat.

'You were leaving me,' he bit at her in hard accusation. 'You were speeding like a crazy woman down that lane because you were leaving me for another man and you got rid of Vance to give yourself a nice clean getaway, only that damn tree got in the way!'

Caught out lying so thoroughly, she felt hot colour rush into her cheeks. His eyes flared as he watched it happen. Defiance rose in response.

'So what if I was?' she tossed back at him. 'What possible difference was it going to make to the way you run your life? We don't have a marriage, we have a business arrangement that I didn't even get to have a say about!' Tears were burning now—hot, angry tears. 'And I dismissed Hugo a week ago, much that you noticed or cared! I have a right to live my own life any way I want—'

'And let another man make love to you any time that you want?'

The raking insert closed Nell's throat, strangling her breath and the denial she could have given in answer to that. Her angry lips followed suit, snapping shut because she didn't want to say it. She did not want to give him anything that could feed his mammoth ego.

The silence between them began to spark like static, his lean face strapped by a fury that stretched his golden skin across the bones in his cheeks as their eyes made war across a gap of barely an inch. Then his other hand came up to cover her throat, light-fingered and gentle but oh, so menacing.

'Say it, *yenika*,' he encouraged thinly. 'Live dangerously...'

He thought she was holding back from admitting she had taken a lover, Nell realised, and felt the triumph in that tingle all the way down to her feet. She moistened her lips—tempted, so desperately tempted that she did not know how she managed to keep the lie back. Their eyes continued to war across several taut, suffocating seconds. It was exciting, knowing that she had the power to shatter his precious ego with a single soft word like *yes*.

The tips of his long fingers moved on her throat, locating a wildly beating pulse. Nell needed to take a breath, her ribs were hurting under the pressure she was placing on them, and in the end she managed a short, tense tug of air into her lungs before improvising shakily, 'If you want to strangle m-me then go ahead; I'm in no fit state to stop you.'

Surprise lit his face. He glanced down to where his fingers curved her throat, dark lashes curling over his eyes before lifting again to view the way his other fingers were knotted into her hair. There was yet another second of taut, breathtaking stillness in which the entire world seemed to grind to a halt. Then the fingers began to slide again, moving almost sensuously against stretched, smooth, creamy flesh as they began to make a slow retreat.

Relief quivered through her, parting her lips on a small, soft gasp. The fingers paused, she held her breath again, felt a different kind of excitement erupt as she flicked a look into the deep, dark, swirling depths of his eyes and saw what she'd always seen there.

Xander had always desired her and Nell had always known it. Whatever else had motivated him into marrying her, the desire had always been the added incentive that made the deal worthwhile.

'You remind me of a sleeping siren,' he murmured. 'It is the only thing that has kept you safe for the last year. Give me one small hint, *cara*, that you have given to someone else that which I have resisted and you will spend the rest of your days regretting it.'

It was just too tempting to resist this time. Defiance back in her eyes, she opened her mouth 'I—'

His mouth arrived to stop whatever she had been about to utter. Shock hit her broadside, sheer surprise at the unexpectedness of it holding her utterly transfixed. He hadn't kissed her once since their wedding night and then he'd been so angry—hard and punishing with frustrated desire. This was different, the anger was still there but the rest was warm, deep and sensually tantalising, the way he used his lips to prise hers apart then stroked the inner recesses of her mouth.

It was her very first tongue-to-tongue experience and the pleasurable sensations it fed into her tapped into one of her many restless, hopeless dreams about moments like this. The warm, clean, expensive scent of him, the smooth, knowing expertise with which he moulded her mouth to his, the slight rasping brush of his skin against her soft skin, the trailing, sensual drag she could feel on her senses that made her relax into him.

He drew back the moment he felt her first tentative response to him. Eyes too dark to read watched the soft quiver of her mouth before he looked deeply into the swirling green confusion mirrored in her eyes. Then he smiled.

'There,' he murmured with silken huskiness. 'I have just saved you from yourself. Aren't you fortunate to have a caring husband like me?'

As she frowned at the comment, he brushed a contemptuous kiss across her still parted mouth then drew right away, fingers trailing from her throat and untangling from her silken hair while she continued to puzzle—until she remembered what she had been about to say before the kiss.

She shivered, horrified at how easily she had let herself be diverted. Resentment poured into her bloodstream. 'I still intend to leave you the moment I get out of here,' she said.

'You will not.' He was already on his feet and replacing the chair back from where he'd got it. 'And I will tell you why.' He sent her a cold look down the length of his arrogant nose. 'We still have a contract to fulfil.'

Nell lifted her chin to him, green eyes wishing him dead now. 'I signed under duress.'

'You mean you signed without reading it.'

Because she'd loved him so much she was blind! 'How many women would expect to be duped by both their own father and their future husband?' she defended her own piece of stupid folly.

Xander nodded in agreement. 'I offered to renegotiate,' he then reminded her. 'You turned the offer down, so the contract stands as written and signed.'

'And all for the love of money,' she said bitterly.

'A loan of fifty million pounds to haul your father out of trouble is a lot of money, Nell. Have you got the resources to pay me back?'

He knew she hadn't. The only money Nell had even a loose connection to was tied up in trusts left by her grandmother for any children Nell might have. And what her mother had left would not even pay back a tenth of what was owed to Xander.

'But I was not referring to the money,' he slid in smoothly. 'I was referring to the other clause—the one which involves me protecting my investment by you providing me with my son and heir to inherit from your father.'

Effectively putting Nell right out of the inheritance loop! 'Not with my permission.'

'With your permission,' he insisted. 'And at my time of choosing…'

He came back to the bed to lean over her again, ignoring her defensive jerk as he began plumping up the pillows behind her back. 'I have been very patient with you until now, *yenika mou*—'

'Because you had more—interesting things to do.'

As a direct shot about Vanessa, it went wide of its mark.

'Because,' he corrected, 'when we married you were nothing but a wounded babe in arms only a monster would have forced himself upon. The arrival of another man on the scene tells me I may well have been too patient with you.' Taking her by the shoulders, he gently urged her to lie back. Then his eyes were pinning her there, relentless and hard. 'Your growing time is up, Nell. I want a proper wife. Renege on the contract we made and I will take you, your father and your boyfriend to the cleaners and hang you all out to dry.'

'And cause yourself a nasty scandal involving yourself, your mistress and your lousy unfaithfulness?'

'Is that why you thought you could leave and get away with it?' Black silk eyebrows made a mocking arch. 'You think that because Vanessa has suddenly arrived back on the scene it gives you a tasty weapon to wield? I will let you into a little secret,' he murmured, a taunting fingertip making a swipe of her full bottom lip before he replaced it with the casual brush of his mouth. 'Vanessa has never been off the scene,' he informed her smoothly. 'I am just very discreet—usually.'

It was like being kicked while she was already down on the ground. It didn't help that her lips had filled with soft, pulsing heat. 'I hope you both rot in hell,' she breathed thickly.

'But you still want me, as that beautiful, quivering, hungry mouth is telling me.' He smiled a very grim smile. 'And if you were not so battered and bruised I would show you how much you want me.'

'I—'

He saw the lie coming, the tight repudiation of his arrogant confidence, and he swooped, claiming her parted mouth and pressing her back into the pillows. The long length of his torso followed, exerting a controlled power that stopped just short of crushing her beneath his weight. Nell felt taken over, overwhelmed, besieged. The scent of him, the heat, the way he used this kiss to demonstrate the difference between taunting and a full sexual onslaught. Hot tingles of sensation flared up from nowhere with the stabbing invasion of his tongue. Fierce heat rushed through her bloodstream, desire like she'd never known before set her groaning in protest and lifting up her hands to push at his chest.

But Xander was going nowhere, the unyielding contours of his body remaining firm as he deepened the kiss with an unhidden hunger that had Nell stretching beneath him in a wild sensual act that arched her slender shape from breasts to toes. He moved with her, a very male thigh finding a place for itself between her thighs. The bedcovers should have lessened the coiling spring of intimacy she was experiencing but did nothing of the kind.

She tried to drag in some air but found that she couldn't. She tried to separate their mouths but he had control. His tongue slid across her tongue and set it quivering as it hungrily began to follow his lead. Nothing had prepared her for a kiss like this. A kiss that sparked senses alive in every intimate place she had. When his hand covered the arching thrust of one of her breasts she almost shattered into little pieces, writhing and gasping as the rosebud nipple stung as it tightened to push into his palm.

He muttered something, went to move away, her hands stopped pushing at his chest and slid up to bury themselves in his hair so she could hold this amazing, sensational mouth clamped to her own. She didn't know she had the ability to behave like a wanton, but wanton she felt and wanton she acted, writhing beneath him, ignoring the many twinges of physical agony because everything else that was happening to her was oh, so much more important. When his thigh pressed into greater contact with the apex of her thighs she went up like tinder, a thick cry of pleasure coiling in her throat.

A knock sounded at the door. Xander drew back like a man bitten. Eyes like burning black coals scorched her a blistering look. Two hot streaks raked his high cheekbones; his mouth pulsed visibly even though it was suddenly stretched taut. She was panting and still clinging to his hair, the green of her eyes glazed by the stunning shock of her own loss of control.

'This had better be your awakening, *cara*, or you're dead,' he blasted down at her, voice rusted by jealous desire.

Before she could construct any kind of answer he had moved away, landing on his feet beside the bed. He did not look at her again until he'd stridden to the door and grasped the handle. The pause he made then sang between them, stretched taut and raw by that final rasping threat.

He was angry—*still* angry. The kiss had been delivered in anger, the deliberate assault of angry passion that left her lying here hot and trembling, shaken to her core by her own response, her mouth, her body, her deserted breast with its stinging nipple feeling utterly, shamefully bereft.

'Hypocrite,' she heard herself whisper across a throat thickened by the bubble of tears to come.

The charge swung him round to lance her with a hard, glinting look. 'And primitive with it,' he extended grimly. 'Forget the lover,' he warned thinly. 'You will not be laying eyes on him again.'

The note in his tone brought Nell upright. 'Why—w-what have you done to him?' she demanded in alarm.

'As yet—nothing.' His eyes blackened dangerously. 'His fate rests in the future when I have more time to discover if he taught you more than just how to kiss.'

Nell blinked then blushed at his thinking behind that revealing comment. He thought it was Marcel who'd taught her to kiss as she'd just done! Her kiss-numb lips parted to speak a denial then closed again. Let his primitive side twist his gut, she thought angrily, lowering her gaze from the piercing hardness of his. Let him learn what it felt like to imagine her locked in naked passion with another man as she had spent the last year imagining him with Vanessa the tramp!

'I will be away for the next few days but will be back in time to collect you from here on Saturday.'

This final piece of news brought her eyes flickering up again as he opened the door and left without another word, allowing whoever had knocked on the door earlier to come into the room.

It was one of his personal bodyguards, his polite greeting spoiled by the tough look on his face. He placed something down on the bedside cupboard. 'Mr Pascalis gave his permission for you to have these,' he said, then went to leave the room.

'H-how long have you been standing out there?' she asked, horrified that he might have heard or—worse—seen what had been going on in here through the little window in the door!

'Since you arrived in this hospital,' Jake Mather replied.

Nell stared at the door closing behind Jake Mather's bulky frame. She'd been under guard without even knowing it. She was in prison. She had been completely surrounded and isolated from the outside world. A shiver shot through her. It was like being back at Rosemere only worse.

Mr Pascalis gave his permission… She turned her head to look at what Xander had kindly given his permission to.

It was a neat stack of papers—tabloids—broadsheets—magazines. Reaching out to pick the top one of the stack, she let it unfold so she could see the front page in all its damning glory. 'Greek tycoon's wife tries to kill herself after he flaunts his mistress.'

No wonder he saw no threat in a scandal—it was already here!

She plucked up another paper and another, swapped them for the magazines. Scandal galore was splashed across the pages. There were even photographs of her wrecked car! She turned the page on those pictures quickly as nausea swam up inside.

But there was no mention of Marcel anywhere, which told her exactly what Xander was doing. Her imprisonment here had nothing to do with contracts or primitive demonstrations of ownership—but with damage control, pure and simple damage control!

He didn't want it reported that his wife had been leaving him for another man when she crashed her car!

He would rather they report that she was attempting to kill herself. What did that say about the size of his ego?

Kill herself? Where had they dragged up that big lie from? Had Xander himself put it out there?

She hated him. Oh, God, she hated him. No wonder she was being so thoroughly isolated. He didn't want her retaliating with the truth!

Leaving him for another man… Oh, how she wished she'd managed to go through with it. She would have written her own headline. 'Wife of philandering Greek tycoon leaves him for Frenchman!'

CHAPTER THREE

STANDING unnoticed in the doorway, Xander watched Nell's trembling fingers grapple with the intricacies of fastening the tiny pearl buttons on the silky white blouse he'd had delivered to her along with a blue linen suit that did amazing things for her slender shape.

Someone had fixed her hair for her and it lay in a thick, shining, sandstorm braid to halfway down her back. She looked very pale, though the bruising on her face had almost disappeared. But it was clear to him that even the simplest of tasks still came as an effort.

She was not recovered, though the doctors had assured him that she was fit to travel and for now that was all he cared about: getting her away from here and to a place void of tabloid gossip—and the temptation to contact her lover the first opportunity she was handed.

His blood began to boil when he thought about the elusive Marcel Dubois. The Frenchman had disappeared into the ether like the scarlet pimpernel, and maybe showed some sense in doing so—sense being something he had not shown when he'd decided to make his play for the wife of Alexander Pascalis.

Wife… He could almost laugh at the title but laughing was not what was lurking inside him. His hooded eyes took on a murderous glitter as he watched Nell struggle with those tiny pearl buttons. Had his wife in name only lain with her Frenchman and allowed him to touch what Xander had not touched? Had Dubois seen power in her soft, willing body and those little confidences a woman like the love-vulnerable Nell would reveal to a lover about the emptiness of her marriage?

She turned then and noticed him standing there. His libido instantly kicked in to join the murderous feelings as her eyes began to make their rise up from his shoes to the casual black brushed-cotton chinos covering his legs and the plain white T-shirt moulding his chest. No other woman had ever looked at him the way Nell looked at him, with a slow, verdant absorption that drenched him in hellishly erotic self-awareness. She could not help herself, he knew that, which made the idea of her giving those looks to another man all the more potent. When she reached his shoulders, covered by the casual black linen jacket he was wearing, he could not halt the small recognising shift of muscle that sent a shower of pleasurable static rushing through his blood.

One day soon he was going to give this awareness true substance, he promised. He was going to wipe out all memory of her other man and introduce her to his power with all its naked, hot passion.

He was no neanderthal; he did not need a woman to be a virgin to enjoy her. But this one, this beautiful freak of modern living with her innocence steeped in womanly desire for him that she still did not have the tools to hide whatever the Frenchman had taught her, was going to open up like a chrysalis under his guidance and fly with him into ecstasy. She owed him that much.

She'd reached his face at last and Xander lost the murderous look to give her the benefit of a slow, easy smile, which she dealt with by flicking her eyes away. Nell was no fool. The last time he was here he had thrown down the sexual gauntlet and the smile was to remind her of it.

'Ready to come with me?' he enquired with the kind of soft challenge that had her breath feathering a quiver across the thrust of her breasts.

'I have no make-up,' she complained. 'You forgot to send it.'

'You don't need make-up. Your beautiful skin does not need it.'

'That's a matter of opinion.' Her chin lifted, eyes pinning him with an arctic green look. 'I've seen the waiting Press out there,' she said with a flick of a hand towards the window.

'Witnessing me leaving here looking black and blue won't help your cause, Xander.'

'And what cause is that?' The sexy smile was beginning to fade, Nell noticed.

'Damage control,' she replied. 'I presumed you would want me to look utterly love-blind and radiant for the cameras.'

'Your tongue is developing an aspish tone that does not suit it,' he drawled, moving further into the room with his graceful stride. 'Can you manage that last button on your blouse or do you need assistance?'

'I can manage.' Her chin dipped, her fingers moving to quickly close the button. 'The fact that I'm unhinged and suicidal does not make me totally useless.'

Xander hooked up her jacket from where it lay on the bed. 'You must admit, Nell, it made hilarious reading.'

'You think it's a big joke?'

'You clearly don't.'

Neither did he by the look on his grim face. The jacket arrived around her slender shoulders, held out absolutely perfectly for her to slide her arms into the sleeves without needing to strain herself.

'They presented me as a spiritless fool.'

'And me as the ruthless womaniser.'

'Better that than a man that cannot keep his wife happy—hmm?'

Nell turned to face him with that aspish challenge, but it was the first time she'd actually stood in front of him in goodness knew how long and it came as a shock to be reminded of his overpowering six feet two inches of pure masculinity compared to her own five feet five inches' more diminutive build.

Black eyes glinted narrowly down at her. 'Are you deliberately goading me into proving you wrong?'

Remembering the kiss of a few days ago, she felt her stomach muscles give a hectic quiver. 'No,' she denied and lowered her eyes in an attempt to block him out as his long fingers smoothed the jacket fabric into place.

'Then take my advice and hold back on the barbs until we can achieve guaranteed privacy.'

As if on cue, the door swung open and the doctor who'd been overseeing her recovery strode into the room. He and Xander shook hands like old friends then proceeded to discuss her as if she wasn't standing right beside them.

So what was new there? Nell asked herself as she stood with her eyes lowered and said not a word. From the moment he'd stepped into it, Xander had been arranging her life for her as if she wasn't a part of it. Their very odd courtship, the contract he had discussed with her father but not with her that she didn't bother to read. The marriage that had taken place in her local church but was put together by his efficient team with very little input from her. So why bother to make a fuss that he was discussing her health with the doctor he'd probably hand-picked to go with the private hospital he'd moved her to without her approval?

The only time he'd ever really listened to her was on their wedding night, when she'd refused to make their marriage real. She might have been upset, angry—hysterical enough to be a turn-off for any man, but she also knew that when he agreed to leave her alone, the final decision had been his. He could have changed her mind. He could have seduced her into weakening to him.

But no, what Xander had done was walk away—easily. Nell cringed inside as she thought it. He'd gone back to his life as if she was not in it, other than for those few token visits aimed to keep up appearances.

As the discussion about her needs went on around her Nell began to feel just a little light-headed because she'd been standing up for longer than she'd done since the accident. Her legs felt shaky and the solid prospect of the nearby chair was almost too tempting to resist. But if she showed signs of weakness now they might decide to keep her here and the risk of being incarcerated for another single hour was enough to keep her stubbornly on her feet.

By the time the doctor turned to say his farewell to her, her fixed smile was wavering though. Xander reached out to take her arm, had to feel the fine tremors shaking her and abruptly cut the goodbyes short.

Two minutes later she was walking down the corridor with his grip like a vice and his grim silence ominous. They entered a lift, the doors closed behind them. Xander propped her up against the wall then remained standing over her as they shot downwards, his grim face strapped by tension. The moment the doors slid open again, he was taking her arm and guiding her out of the lift.

Nell showed a brief start of surprise when she realised they had not arrived in the hospital foyer but in a basement car park and she had never felt so relieved about anything. Not only had Xander pre-empted the Press pack but his black Bentley stood parked right there in front of them with Jake Mather standing to attention by the open rear door.

Nell sank with trembling relief into soft leather. The door closed as another opened. Xander arrived at her side and within seconds they were on the move.

So what came next? she wondered wearily when, a short minute later, Xander was on his mobile phone, lean dark profile wearing its power mask as he talked in smooth, liquid Italian then switched to rich, sensual Greek for the second call he made.

Uttering a small sigh, she closed her eyes and just let the sound of his voice wash over her—only to open them again with a start when her door came open and she found herself blinking owlishly at Xander, who was leaning into the car and unlocking her seat belt.

She must have fallen asleep. As she was too disoriented to do more than let him help her out of the car, it took a few more seconds for her brain to register that she was not standing outside Rosemere.

'What's going on?' she questioned.

'Nothing.' With a coolness that belied the alarm that was beginning to erupt inside her, he turned her round so she could see the sleek white private jet standing on tarmac a few yards away. 'We are going home, that's all.'

'By air?' She blinked again as he drew her across those few yards towards the waiting flight steps. 'But it's only an hour by car back to Rose—'

'Greece,' he corrected. 'I need to be in Athens on Monday morning, and if you think I am leaving you alone at Rosemere to plot assignations with your Frenchman then think again.'

Greece, Nell repeated and stopped dead at the entrance to the plane. Her heart gave a punch against her sore ribs. 'No,' she refused. 'I don't want to go—'

'Don't make a fuss, *agapita*.' The flat of his hand at the base of her spine gave her a gentle push forward. Before she knew it, she'd been hustled inside the plane and the door was being closed.

Staring bemusedly at her luxury surroundings, she turned suddenly to make a protest and cannoned right into Xander's chest. The breath left her body on a tense little whoosh and she tried to take a defensive step back, but his arms came around her, strong and supportive. It was like being surrounded by the enemy, frightening and suffocating.

She breathed in anxious protest. 'Please…'

'Please what?'

His voice had deepened and roughened. Glancing up, Nell saw the dark, simmering spark in his eyes and tried one final breathless, 'No…'

But his mouth found hers anyway, moulding her lips and prising them apart to allow his tongue to make that slow, sensual slide against moist inner tissue that made her breath quiver as her senses tingled with pleasure. She wanted to pull away but instead her mouth crushed in closer. She wanted to deny this was happening at all but once again her mind was not in control. He murmured something, she didn't know what. But his tongue when it delved deeper sent her hands up to clutch at his chest and, as strong male muscle rippled beneath her fingers, he eased her even closer to him.

His thighs pressed against her thighs, the solid evidence of his desire pushing against the tense flatness of her lower stomach. Damp heat sprang out all over her and on a very masculine growl he deepened the kiss some more. Dizzily she clung to him, her breathing coming faster as the intensity of the kiss increased. Her head tilted backwards, arching her breasts into the solid wall of his chest. Her nipples sharpened like stinging arrows against him and she could feel the uneven thump of his heart and the fine tremor attacking him as he used long fingers to draw her more tightly against the sensual movements he was making with his hips. It was all so sexual, so overwhelmingly physical and exciting. A shimmering, quivering shower of desire dragged at inner muscles that seemed to scoop out the strength from her legs.

Then the plane's engines gave a sudden roar, breaking them apart with an abruptness that left Nell staring dizzily up at his face. She saw the tension there, heat streaking across his cheekbones, the flaring nostrils, the predatory burn in his eyes, and quivered out a constricted gasp.

He dipped his dark head and caught the sound, burnt this kiss onto her pulsing lips—then without warning took hold of her shoulders, turned and dumped her unceremoniously into the nearest seat then spun away in an odd jerky movement that kept her eyes fixed on him in giddy fascination.

He really wanted her. Badly. Now. The knowledge ploughed a deep furrow of heat down her front and held her utterly, breathlessly entrapped. When he suddenly twisted back round to look at her his eyes were so black she didn't even try to look for the brown. That one glance at her expression and he was growling out some kind of harsh self-aimed curse and coming down on his haunches to grimly belt her in. Her eyes clung to his taut features as he did so. She didn't even breathe when he moved away to take a seat on the other side of the aisle and strapped himself into it.

Nothing going on inside was making any sense to her any more; everything was just too new. The plane engines gave another roar then they were shooting forward with rocket propulsion that only helped to heighten the awareness pulsing back and forth.

'If you ever let another man touch you again I will kill you,' he rasped into the charged atmosphere.

Kill her—kill Marcel. The primitive man in him was beginning to take on a life of his own. Is this what untrammelled lust did to men—turned them all into angry, murderous, primeval beasts?

'Speak!' Xander lashed out, stopping her thought processes stone dead as he seared a blistering look across the aisle.

He wanted her to retaliate. To spit something back at him about Vanessa so he could shoot her down with some cruel remark. It was all to do with a need to finding an alternative release for all of this tension, but she turned her face away and refused to respond.

Couldn't respond; she was too locked up inside with what she was feeling herself.

They were already in the air and still shooting higher; the pressure in the cabin hummed in her head. Lifting a set of trembling fingers, she touched the place above her nose where the last and worst bruise on her face still lingered. She thought it would be throbbing, it felt as if it was but it was all over that was throbbing.

A click followed by an angry hissing sound came at her from across the aisle and she dropped the fingers back to her lap—only to find that Xander had moved with the speed of light, unfastening his belt to come to squat down in front of her again, his own long, cool fingers coming up to cover where her own had just covered.

'You are hot and in pain,' he muttered angrily. 'I apologise for my—thoughtlessness.'

Sounding stiff and very foreign to her now, 'I'm all right,' she managed on a shaken breath.

'You are not.' His fingers moved to one of her burning cheeks. 'Don't give me that stiff upper-lip stuff, Nell. I treated you roughly. You now think I am crass and uncivilised,' he brusquely pronounced. 'Did I hurt you anywhere—your injured ribs?'

Nell reached up to curl her fingers around his wrist to pull it away from her cheek so she could give a negating shake of her head and was instantly assailed by the sensation of strong bone and warm skin peppered with crisp dark hair. This was mad, she tried to swallow, found her eyes lifting to clash with his. Darkened emerald-green showing a complete helplessness as to what was happening to her. She'd spent so many months blocking out what she used to feel for him; now it was all pounding about inside her and she didn't like it.

She tugged her hand down again. 'Let me go home to Rosemere,' she whispered unsteadily.

'No.' It came out hard and gruff. 'Where I go you go from now on. I want you with me.' Eyes no longer black with passion but dark—dark brown and swirling with feelings that shattered the breath she tried to take.

'So you can protect your investment?' she hit out. 'Your bodyguards can do that just as well in England.'

'So I believed. You proved me wrong.' He sprang to his feet. 'We will not discuss this again.'

She only had herself to blame for what was happening to her now, in other words. She looked away from him, and had never felt so trapped in her life.

They landed in Athens to a blistering heatwave that almost sucked her of her remaining strength as they transferred to a waiting helicopter and immediately took off again. Three and a half hours on a plane, too much tension and stress, and she was beginning to feel so wiped out she could barely sit up straight.

'Where to now?' she asked as they swung out over a glistening blue ocean with this now daunting man at the controls.

'To my private island.'

Spoken like a true Greek billionaire, with an indifference that suggested that all Greeks owned their own island. Nell was too tired to do more than grimace at his arrogance.

But she couldn't stop the tip of her tongue from running an

exploratory track across her still warm and swollen full bottom lip, unaware that Xander witnessed the revealing little gesture and the way he had to clench hard on a certain part of his anatomy to stop the hot response from gaining in strength.

The island turned out to be a tiny baked brown circle of land floating alone in a crystal blue ocean. Nell caught sight of two white crescents of sand, a fir-covered hill in the middle, and a beautiful two-storeyed whitewashed villa with a swimming pool nestling in between the two sandy beaches.

They landed in an area close to the pool. Jumping out, Xander had to stoop as he strode round to the other side of the machine to open her door, then held out his hand to help her alight. She stumbled as he hurried her from beneath the rotors. A sharp frowning glance at the exhaustion wrenching at her pale face and he was scooping her off the ground.

'I can walk—'

'If you had to,' he agreed tersely. 'Which you don't.'

With a sigh, Nell gave in because she didn't have the energy to argue with him never mind the strength to put up a physical fight. Her head lolled onto his shoulder, his warm breath brushed her face as he carried her past the glinting blue pool and up a set of wide, shallow steps towards the house. A wall of plate-glass stood open ready for them and a tiny woman dressed in black waited to welcome them with a warm, crinkly smile.

She said something in Greek. Xander answered in the same language, his tone short and clipped. The old woman lost her smile and turned to hurry inside ahead of them, tossing long sentences over her shoulder that sounded to Nell as if Xander was being thoroughly scolded, like a child. He seemed to take it without objection, allowing the woman to lead the way across a cool hallway and up a flight of stairs.

They entered a beautiful room with pale blue walls and white drapes billowing at the floor-length windows covered by blue slatted shutters that helped to keep out the worst of the afternoon heat. Setting Nell down on the edge of a pale blue covered soft, springy bed, Xander clipped out an order and the woman hurried away, leaving him squatting down in front of Nell, whose head was just too heavy to lift off his shoulder.

'The journey was too much,' he hissed. 'I apologise.'

Again? Nell thought. 'I just want to go to bed.'

At any other time Xander would have jumped on such an appealing statement. But not right now, when it was clear she was totally wasted and he was worried and feeling as guilty as hell for putting her through such a journey before she had recovered her strength.

Reaching between them, he unbuttoned the lightweight blue summer jacket and slid it carefully from her shoulders then tossed it aside. The white blouse was silky, the tiny pearl buttons more difficult to negotiate from this position and he frowned as his fingers worked, the frown due more to her silent acquiescence. It was a good ten seconds before he realised that she'd actually fallen asleep.

The blouse came free and landed on top of the jacket, working by stealth, he gently laid her down against the pillows then shifted his attention to removing her shoes then the slippery silk-lined skirt and lace-edged stockings that covered her slender legs. Leaving her dignity intact with her lacy bra and panties, he was just grimacing to himself because this was as naked as he had ever seen his wife of a year—when he saw what he had missed while he'd been busy undressing her and it straightened his spine with a stark, rigid jerk.

She was so badly bruised he could not believe the doctor had dared to say that she was fit to travel! One whole side of her ribcage was a mass of fading purple and yellow, and he just stared in blistering horror at the two thick seat-belt lines, one that ran from her left shoulder diagonally across her body to her waist, where the other took over, strapping straight across her hips.

What the hell kind of speed had she been doing when she hit that tree to cause such bruising?

Had it been deliberate?

His blood ran cold at an idea he dismissed instantly. But the cold shock of the thought lingered much longer than that. And the guilt he had been feeling at the rough way he'd handled her on the plane grew like a balloon in his chest.

Someone tutted beside him. 'Oh, poor wounded child,' Thea Sophia murmured. 'What kind of man have you become, Alexander, that you bring her this far in this state?'

It was not a question he cared to answer. He was struggling enough with it for himself. Setting his mouth, he bent down to gather Nell into his arms again with as much care as he could manage.

'Pull back the covers, Thea,' he instructed gruffly. Ten seconds later he was resettling his wounded bride against the cool sheets of their marriage bed.

Did she but know it, he thought as he straightened a second time and stepped back to allow Thea to gently fold the covers back over Nell's limp frame. Her hair lay in a thick braid beside one of her cheeks and she had never looked so pale—or so vulnerable.

God give me strength, he thought grimly, glad that only he knew what plans he'd made for the beautiful Helen involving this island, some serious seduction, this room and this bed.

Shelved plans. He turned away, grim face mask-like as he watched Thea fuss around picking up Nell's discarded clothes and folding them neatly on a chair.

He made a decision. One of those quick-thinking, business-minded decisions he was more familiar with. It was called a tactical retreat.

Nell slept on through the sound of rotor blades stirring up again, slept through the whooshing din the helicopter made as it took off. She had no idea at all that while she slept Thea Sophia sat in the chair beside the bed, quietly working her lace with gnarled, nimble fingers while a maid just as quietly unpacked and put away Nell's clothes. The afternoon sun slowly turned the room golden. She only stirred when the sound of rattling crockery made her dry throat and her empty stomach demand she take note.

Opening her eyes, she took several long seconds to remember where she was, and a few more seconds' sleepily watching the old lady in black as she fussed around a table by the window across the room. Then the old lady turned.

'Ah, you are awake at last!' she exclaimed and came across the room with her crinkly face full of olive-toned smiles. 'My name is Sophia Theodora Pascalis,' she introduced herself. 'I am Alexander's great-aunt. You may call me Thea Sophia and I will call you Helen—such a proud Greek name.'

Was it? Nell had never given much thought to her name's origin.

'Of course, if Alexander were here he would have made the formal introductions,' Thea Sophia continued. 'But welcome— welcome to our beautiful island and our beautiful home, Helen.' Nell found her face being clasped between two hands in a warm, affectionate gesture, and released again.

'Th-thank you. I'm very happy to meet you, Thea Sophia,' Nell returned politely and it was impossible not to smile back in response.

'Ah, it is I who is happy to see you here at last.' The old lady stood back to beam a very satisfied smile then turned to walk back to the table by the window. 'We will become very good friends, you and I, *ne*? You will like it here,' she promised. 'When that stupid boy Alexander decides to get his priorities right and come back here you will makes lots of babies between you in that bed as is Pascalis tradition and we shall be a very happy family, *ne*?'

The baby part floated right by Nell, pushed out by the much more disturbing part of Thea Sophia's chatty speech. 'Xan— Alexander has…gone?' she prompted unsteadily.

'He took one look at your poor bruised body and took to his heels,' his aunt informed her in disgust. 'You would not believe that such a big strong man could be so squeamish, but there you go.' She added a very Mediterranean shrug. 'It will be his guilty conscience taunting him, of course. He was brought up to protect his loved ones. In this, with you, he failed. He will come back when he has come to terms with his…'

Nell had stopped listening. She was pushing the covers away from her body and staring down at her near-naked flesh. Hot colour poured into her cheeks then paled away again when she saw what Xander had seen.

'W-who undressed me?'

'Alexander, of course.'

'Then he left…'

'*Ne.*' China chinked against china.

Nell sat up with a jerk and drew her knees up to her chin so that she could hug herself. Tears were burning, hurt tears, angry tears.

Xander had brought her to this island to seduce her—he'd left Nell in no doubt whatsoever about that. One glance at her miserable body and he'd seen his plans thwarted so he'd done what he always did.

He'd walked away. Left her. Marooned her on this tiny island with this sweet but *old*, old lady, while he returned to his busy, important life, the seduction of his wife shelved—again.

'You ready for a nice cup of English tea now…?'

CHAPTER FOUR

NELL stepped barefooted onto the sand, dropped her book and her sunglasses down at her feet then removed the wide-brimmed straw hat Thea Sophia had insisted that she wear to shade her face from the fierce rays of the sun.

Using the hat as a fan, she wafted it to and fro as she stood looking around the small cove she'd found during her first week here and since then made it her very own. It meant a stiff climb up and down the tree-covered hill to get here but it was worth it. The sand beneath her feet was sugary soft and hot, the sea a crystal-clear, smooth as glass, glistening blue, and in between the two lay a strip of cooler damp-silk sand kept that way by the flow and ebb of a lazy tide.

It was the stillest day since she had arrived here two weeks ago. Hot, breathlessly calm, exotically pine-scented and so exquisitely hush-quiet you could hear an ant move a leaf fifty feet away.

A wry smile played with her mouth as she stooped over again to place the hat over the book and sunglasses, paused long enough to scoop up a handful of warm sand then straightened again, green eyes fixed thoughtfully on her fingers as she let the sand filter through them while she tried to decide what she was going to do.

She was being watched. Not only was she very aware of that pair of eyes fixed on her, but she also knew to whom they belonged. She'd heard the helicopter fly overhead as she'd been strolling up the path that led over the pine-shaded hill on her way here. She also knew how he had found her so quickly. Yannis, the bluff, gruff odd-job man on the island and her latest guard would have told him where to look.

It made her curious as to whether it had ever occurred to

Xander that having her watched for every waking hour of the day meant that Yannis often saw what he was seeing right now as he stood beneath the shade of one of the trees that edged the little cove.

If her instincts were sending her the right messages, that was, and she knew that they were. Only one man had ever filled her with this tingling mix of anger, resentment and excitement just by looking at her.

There were two things she could do next, she pondered thoughtfully. She could turn round and confront him or she could ignore him and continue with what she'd come here to do.

The smile on her lips stretched wider. It was not a pleasant smile. The first option had never been a real contender, Nell had known it from the moment she'd heard his first footfall on the woodland path behind. There was no way that she was going to turn and let him know that she knew he was standing there.

It did not suit her purposes because she was about to show him just what it was he had been consistently rejecting for the last year. Show him how she looked without the bruises he'd turned his back on in favour of Athens and probably Vanessa's perfect, unblemished, *willing* charms.

Her fingers shook a little, though, as she began to untie the knot holding her sarong in place across the warm rise of her breasts. Her heart pumping a bit too thickly as she let the fine white Indian cotton slide away from her body to land softly on the top of the hat.

Underneath the sarong the new honey-gold tan she had been carefully cultivating shone softly beneath a protective layer of high-factor oil. Exercising three times a day by swimming in the pool or here in the sea had toned her up quite impressively—not that she'd been a slouch before the accident, but physical injury had taken a toll on her weight and her muscles.

Now, as she stood looking down at herself, a lazy finger absently rubbing in a previously missed smear of oil across the flat slope of her stomach, she was quietly impressed with how she looked even if it was vain to think it about herself. Whoever it was who'd packed her clothes for her in England must have been in romantic mood because they'd more or less picked out everything she'd bought for her non-starter honeymoon, like this bikini for instance, bought along with several others to seduce a husband who should have been her lover by the time she'd worn one of them.

The bikini consisted of a tiny white G-string that made only a scornful play at covering what it should, and a skimpy top made of two tiny triangles of silky fabric held together by two bootlace straps, one knotted around her neck and the other around her back. If she swam too energetically she came out of the top but—who cared? she thought with a large dose of defiance. She felt slinky and sexy and the G-string wasn't going to go anywhere because of the way it was held in place in the tight cleft of her buttocks.

So eat your heart out, Alexander Pascalis, she told him as she tilted her face up to the sun. Because here stands the unbattered version of the woman you turned your back on two weeks ago. And on that rebellious thought she moved into a long, slow, sensual stretch that accentuated every slender line of her figure from arms to spine to smoothly glossed buttocks and long, slender legs, held the pose for a few seconds then released it and began running lightly down to the sea.

In the shade of the tree, Xander watched the start of her little exhibition from a lazy, relaxed stance with one shoulder resting against the tree trunk.

She knew he was here, he was almost certain of it. She had to have heard his footfall on the path on such a still day. So, what was she thinking about as she stood there sifting sand through her fingers? Was she contemplating how he would react to a handful of the sand thrown in his face?

He knew she was angry with him. He knew she felt dumped and deserted when he'd left her here the way that he did. But what other choice had he had at the time? He had a wife who was not yet a wife and a marriage bed that was not yet a marriage bed that his aunt fully expected them to share.

Playing the loving husband who'd had a whole year to lose the edge to his sexual desires for this woman had not been an option he had been able to take. Put him in a bed next to Nell and despite the bruises he would not have been able to keep his hands to himself.

She was beautiful—look at her, he told that nagging part of his conscience that kept on telling him he could have sorted something out which had not involved shifting himself across the Aegean in a bid to put temptation out of reach.

The long, slender legs, the slender body hidden beneath the white sarong she had tied round the firm thrust of her breasts. The pale copper hair left free to ripple across slender shoulders tanned to a smooth honey colour since he'd seen them last.

Turn to look at me, *yenika*, he urged silently. Give me that slow, sensual glide with your eyes that turns up my sexual heat. I don't mind paying the price of the sand in my face.

But she didn't turn. Leaning there against the tree while willing the little witch to turn, Xander watched through eyes narrowed against the sunlight as she untied the knot holding the sarong in place then allowed the scrap of fine white Indian cotton to slide away from her body and fall on top of the hat.

His heart stopped beating. His shoulder left the tree trunk with a violent jerk. He could not believe what he was seeing. In fact he refused to believe it. It was the sun playing tricks with his eyes, he decided as he watched her move into a long, lithe stretch, which lifted her arms up as if in homage to the sun.

'*Theos,*' he breathed as his senses locked into overdrive. He'd seen many women in many different stages of undress. He'd seen them deliberately playing the temptress in an effort to capture his interest but he never expected to see this woman do it—never expected to see her wearing anything so damned outrageous!

Maybe she did not know of his presence. Maybe she was playing the siren like this because she truly believed there was no one to see!

Then he remembered Yannis—warned to follow her every

move because he did not trust her not to find some way to flee again. The idea of any other man enjoying the sight of his wife parading herself in what could only be called a couple of pieces of string had a red-hot tide of primitive possessiveness raking through him and sent his head shooting round, glinting black eyes flashing out a scan around the area, hunting out places a silent guard could watch unseen.

Then she dropped out of the stretch and his attention became riveted on Nell again as she began to run down to the sea, light steps kicking up soft, dry sand then leaving small footprints in the wet as she went. She hit the water at a run, her beautiful hair flying out behind her. In a smooth, graceful, curving dive, she disappeared beneath the smooth crystal water, leaving him standing there hot, damp in places, feeling as if he had just imagined the whole thing!

Nell swam beneath the surface until her lungs began to burst then she bobbed up like a seal, took in a deep breath then struck out with a smooth, graceful crawl towards the edge of the little cove where the rocky landscape on this side of the island rose up in a sheer slab for several feet she'd always thought would be great to dive from but had not yet found a way to reach the edge up there.

The tiny cove was perfect for swimming in because its two flanking outcrops gave her something to aim for when she swam across the cove. Making a neat racing turn, she started back in the other direction. She loved swimming, always had from being small. She'd swum for her school and won a few gold medals too. In Canada she'd scared her mother by swimming in the Kananaskis River, and before getting married had been a regular visitor to the local public swimming pool. When she'd married Xander, he had changed all of that by closeting her at Rosemere, which had its own pool, so she did not have to leave home to swim. On the rare occasions he'd turned up at the house unexpectedly to find her using the pool, she'd glimpsed him standing by the bevelled glass doors watching her cut a smooth line through the water—not that she'd ever let him know that she'd known he was standing there. When you hated and resented someone you ignored them as much as possible then they could never know what was really fizzing around your insides.

She made sure she did not look his way now, though the fact that she knew he was there watching her filled her with a mad, crazy, excited exhilaration as she cut through the water with smooth, darting strokes that barely caused a ripple on the ocean surface.

She was halfway across the cove when he struck, swimming beneath her and closing his hands around her waist. Nell let out a shrill, high-pitched scream and almost drowned as she gulped salt water into her lungs just before Xander lifted her high out of the water, rising like a big, black-eyed Poseidon out of the sea with his catch gripped between his hands.

'You shameless, ruthless provocateur!' he bellowed at her, then brought her sliding down the length of his body until her face was level with his.

Still coughing and choking, and almost hyperventilating with shock, Nell felt her skin slither against hard, tough, hair-roughened skin, legs, breast—*hips*! 'Oh, my God,' she gasped out. 'You've got no clothes on!'

'*I* have no clothes on?' he bit out angrily. 'What the hell do you think it is that *you* are wearing?'

Clutching at his satin-tight shoulders because she had to clutch at something, Nell lowered her eyes from the fury burning in his, then wished she hadn't when she saw to her horror that the two wet triangles of silk that should be covering her breasts had shifted and now two tight pink nipples were pouting at her like reckless taunts. Colour pouring into her wet cheeks, she flicked her wide eyes back to his blazing eyes and opened her mouth to retaliate with something—but he got there first, slamming his mouth onto hers with all the angry passion that had driven him through the water, submerged and unseen until he could grab her from underneath.

It was a kiss like nothing she had ever experienced. Open-mouthed, hot, frenzied and deep. It didn't help that they were both still panting from their energetic swim, both hearts pounding like thunder, both straining wildly against each other, her fingernails digging into his shoulders, his like clamps around her slippery waist.

The rough sound of masculine desire ground from his throat and he broke the kiss to lift her high again, eyes like burning black coals as he dipped his head and latched his mouth onto one of her breasts. The greedy suck dragged a shocked cry of pleasure from her, and sent him in search of the other breast.

When he lowered her to recapture her mouth he moved his hands to her wriggling hips, used long, sensually sliding fingers to urge uselessly flailing legs apart then wrapped them firmly around his hips. She took the new intimacy with a breath-gulping quiver, felt the bold thrust of his penis, rock-solid and probing against her flesh. The G-string was no barrier. She was going to lose her virginity right here in the ocean to a man balanced on the edge between violence and passion, and what was worse, she didn't care.

His hands were moulding the tight curve of her bottom now, her fingers buried in the wet silk of his hair, fingernails clawing at his scalp. The kiss was so wild and hot and urgent she felt dizzy from it, then it was gone.

With an angry growl he thrust her from him, sending her floundering into the sea. She dropped beneath the surface. By the time she'd gathered enough sense to make the push back to the surface he was already pounding his way back to the beach.

It was the worst, most devastating rejection he had ever dealt her. For a horrible few seconds Nell thought she was going to faint. If she could she would be turning and swimming out to sea just to get away from the fresh burn of rejection she was feeling but he'd sapped her strength, taking it with him like some lethal, heartless virus, leaving her with this hot, sensual, dragging feeling that was so new to her she didn't know what to do to ease herself out of its grip.

She watched him rise out of the water, a beautiful, wide-shouldered, long-bodied, bronze-skinned male without a hint of shame in his own nakedness. Toned muscles that moved and flexed in lithe coordination were caught to perfection by the water clinging to his flesh and the loving glint of the sun. He did not look back, and Nell could feel his anger emanating towards her back across the calm ocean and she hated herself for responding to him. Her breasts felt heavy, their tips tingling and tight. Even as she trod water in an effort to keep herself afloat her thighs had clamped together as if to hold in their first experience of a fully aroused man thrusting against the hidden flesh.

It took every bit of will-power she could drum up to make herself follow him, dipping beneath the water in an effort to cool the heat from her face and her body then angrily resettling her bikini top before she allowed herself to surface again then make deeply reluctant strikes for the shore.

By the time she reached it he'd pulled on a pair of smooth-fitting trousers, muscles clenching tightly across his glistening back when he heard the splash of her feet as she waded through the shallows to the beach.

Bending down, he scooped up her sarong, half turned and tossed it to her. It landed in a floaty drift of white on the damp sand at her feet, and he was already snatching up his shirt and dragging it on over his glinting wet skin.

Xander thought about apologising but he'd played that hand before and too often to give the words any impact. Anyway, he was not sorry. He was angry and aroused and he could still feel her legs wrapped around him, could still taste her in his mouth. He had an ache between his legs that was threatening to envelop him.

'You will not flaunt your body in get-ups like that excuse for a bikini,' he clipped out, heard the words, realised he sounded like a disapproving father, hated that, uttered a driven sigh that spun him about.

She was trying to knot the sarong with fumbling fingers. Her beautiful hair was slicked to her head. She had never looked more subdued or more tragic.

'And when we get around to making love it will not be out in the open for anyone to watch us,' he heard himself add.

'Behind a locked bedroom door on a bed, maybe,' she suggested. 'How boringly conventional of you.'

Subdued but not dead, Xander noted from that little piece of slicing derision. He could not help the smile that twitched at his mouth. It eased some of the passion-soaked aggression out of his voice.

'More comfortable too,' he agreed drily. 'I was treading water out there. I don't know how I kept us both floating. Add some of the really physical stuff and I would likely have drowned us in the process.'

'I can swim.'

'Not with me deep inside you, *agape mou*,' he drawled lazily. 'Trust me, you would have lost the will to live rather than let me go.'

She managed the knot. He had a feeling it cut off the circulation, it appeared so tight. And her cheeks went a deep shade of pink. He liked that. However, the look she sent him should have shrivelled his ego like a prune. It didn't though. The physical part of his ego remained very much erect and full.

'Such confidence in your prowess,' she mocked, stalking past him to scoop up the rest of her things. 'Don't they always say that those who boast about it always disappoint?'

'I will not disappoint,' he assured with husky confidence.

'Well, if you wait until it's dark to prove that, I can always pretend you are someone else, then maybe you won't.'

And with the pithy comment to cut him down to size where he stood she put the hat on her head and walked off towards the path.

A lesser man would react to such an insult. A lesser man, Xander told himself as he watched her walk away, would go after her and drag her down in the sand and make her take such foolish words back.

The better man picked up his socks and shoes and followed her at a leisurely pace, while he plotted his revenge by more—subtle methods.

Then a frown creased his smooth brow when he remembered something and increased his pace, only becoming leisurely again once he'd caught up with her and tempered his longer stride to hers.

Hearing him coming, Nell pushed her sunglasses over her burning eyes and increased her pace. She received a glimpse of sun-dappled white shirting, black trousers and a pair of long brown bare feet as he came up beside her, but her mind saw the naked man and her tummy muscles fluttered. So did other parts.

'I grew up on this island,' he remarked casually. 'As a small boy I used to walk this path each morning to swim in the cove before being shipped across to the mainland to attend school. Diving from the rocks is an exhilarating experience. The snorkelling is good out there, the fishing too—though I do not suppose the fishing part is of any interest to you.'

'You, used to fish?' Nell spoke the words without thinking then was angry because she'd been determined to say nothing at all.

'You think I arrived on this earth all-powerful and arrogant?' He mocked her lazily. 'In the afternoons I used to fish,' he explained. 'Having been transported back here after my school day was finished, with my ever-present bodyguard as my only playmate.'

Now he was playing on her sympathies by drawing heart-string-plucking pictures of a small, lonely boy protected and isolated from the world because of his father's great power and wealth.

'My parents were always off somewhere doing important things so I rarely saw them,' he went on. 'Thea Sophia brought me up, taught me good manners and the major values of life. The fishing taught me how to survive on my own if I had to. I used to worry constantly that something dreadful was going to happen to those who lived here on the island with me and I would be left alone here to fend for myself. I knew that my father had powerful enemies that might decide to use me in their quest for revenge. Before the age of six I had all my hiding places picked out for when they came for me...'

'Is there a point to you telling me this?' She would not feel sorry for that small, anxious boy, she wouldn't.

'*Ne.*' He slipped into Greek, which didn't happen often.

Xander was a man of many languages. Greek and Italian both being natural to him, the rest because he was good at them, and in the cut-throat, high-risk world he moved in it paid to know what the people around you were saying and to be able to communicate that fact.

'You think that you are the only one to have lived a strange, dysfunctional, sheltered life but you are not,' he stated coolly. 'I have lived it too so I can recognise the person you are inside because I am familiar with that person.'

Nell clutched her book in tight fingers and tried hard not to ask the question he was prompting her to ask, but it came out anyway. 'And what kind of person is that?'

'One who hides her true self within a series of carefully constructed shells as a form of self-defence against the hurts, the fears, the rejections life has dealt her from being small and vulnerable—like myself.'

Well, he certainly knows how to top up my feelings of rejection! Nell thought angrily. 'What rubbish,' she snapped out loud. 'And spare me more of this psycho-babble, Xander. I have no idea where you're going with it and I don't want to know.'

'Towards a deeper understanding of each other?' he suggested.

'For what purpose? So you can eventually get around to bedding me before you fly off to pastures new—or old,' she tagged on with bite. 'In case you didn't notice, I was easy prey out there in the water.' God, it stung to have to admit that. 'That means you don't need to achieve a greater understanding of me to get what you want.'

'You have always been easy prey, *cara*,' he hit back. 'The point at issue here is that I have always managed to avoid taking what has always been there to take.'

Nell pulled to a simmering stop. The hat and the sunglasses

hid her expression from him but there were other ways to transmit body language. 'I think you're into humiliation.'

'No,' he denied that. 'I was trying to…'

She walked on again, faster, her breath singing tensely from between her clenched teeth as she pumped her legs up the final stretch of the hill.

'Will you listen to me?' He arrived at her side again.

'Listen to you spelling it out for me that you married me because you saw your perfect soul mate? One you can pick up and drop at will and she won't complain because she's used to rejection, and all of this rotten isolation you prefer to surround her with?'

'I married you,' he gritted, 'because it was either that or take you to bed without the damned ring!'

Her huff of scorn echoed high in the trees above them. 'I was a business deal!' She turned on him furiously, brought her foot down on a sharp piece of gravel and let out a painful, 'Ouch!'

'What have you done?' he rasped.

'Nothing.' She rubbed at the base of her foot with a hand. 'And we've never shared a bed!' she flashed at him furiously. 'We've never even shared a bedroom!'

'Well, that's about to change,' he drawled.

I'm not listening to any more, Nell decided and dropped her foot to the ground to turn and start walking again, her legs and her body trembling with fury and goodness knew what else while her eyes still saw a tall, dark, *arrogant* man with tousled wet hair and a sexy damp shirt, dangling his shoes from his long brown fingers.

Topping the peak of the hill, she started down the other side of it. Below through the trees she could see the red-tiled roof of the house and the helicopter standing in its allotted spot by a glinting blue swimming pool.

All looked idyllic, a perfect haven of peace—sanctuary.

Sanctuary to hell! she thought. Her sanctuary had been in the isolation, not the place itself. Now Xander was back and the comfortable new world she'd created here was shattered.

She hated him so much it was no wonder her blood was fizzing like crazy as it coursed through her veins.

He did it again and took her by surprise, hands snaking around her waist to spin her round to face him. The shoes had landed with a clunk somewhere, her book went the same way. Next thing her hat came off, followed by her sunglasses, and were tossed aside. She caught a fleeting glimpse of a lean, dark, handsome face wearing the grim intent of what was to come, her breath caught on a gasp then that hard, hot mouth was claiming hers again and she was being kissed breathless while his hands roamed at will.

Her thighs, her hips, the smooth, rounded curve of her naked bottom beneath the covering sarong. He staked his claim without conscience, her slender back, her flat stomach, the still thrusting, pouting shape of her nipple-tight breasts. She was dizzy, narcotic, clinging to him, fingers clawing inside the shirt to bury into the tightly curling matt of hair on his chest.

It had all erupted without a warning gap now, as if one erotic encounter led straight into the next. He drew back from the kiss, face hardened by a burning desire that was no longer held in check.

'You want that we do it right here and now, Nell—up against the nearest tree maybe?' he gritted down at her. 'Or shall we go back to the ocean and complete what we started there? Or would you have preferred it if we had done it two weeks ago in the bed down there where you lay injured and weak? Or we could have whiled away the hours doing it on the flight over here. Or let us take this back to our wedding night, when you were so shattered only a monster would have tried. No,' he ground out. 'You will not turn away from me.'

His hands snaked her closer, cupping her behind to lift her into even closer contact. 'Do you understand now what I am trying to say to you? Look at us, *cara*,' he insisted. 'We are not what you would call passive about this. You hide your true self. I hide my true self. But here they are out in the open, two people with more passion for each other than they can safely deal with.'

'Only when you have the time to feel like it.'

'Well, I feel like it now!' he rasped. 'And if you refuse to listen to reason then maybe I will take you up against a tree, with your knees trapped beneath my arms and your heels digging into my back!'

Such a lurid, vivid picture made her push back from him, all big, shocked green eyes. 'You've done it before like that!'

Xander laughed—thickly, so thoroughly disconcerted by the attack that he discovered he had no defence.

The whooshing sound of a helicopter's rotor blades suddenly sounded overhead, saving him from having to defend himself. They both looked up then Xander uttered a thick curse.

'We have a visitor,' he muttered.

'Who?' Nell shot out as they watched the helicopter swoop down the side of the hill then come to a hovering stop beside the other one.

There was a moment of nothing, a moment of hovering stillness in Xander that brought her eyes back to his face. He didn't look happy. He even sent her a grimace.

'My mother,' he said.

CHAPTER FIVE

His mother…

Nell's heart sank to the soles of her bare feet. The beautiful, gorgeous, always exquisitely turned out Gabriela Pascalis was paying them a visit and Nell looked like this—wet, bedraggled, and more than half-ravished.

Her voice developed a shake. 'Did you know she was coming here?'

There was a sighed-out, 'No,' before he changed it to a heavy, 'Yes… She said she was coming. I told her not to bother. I knew she would ignore me—all right?'

Nell flashed him a killing look. 'You didn't think to warn me about that?'

'We were busy talking about other things—I forgot.'

He forgot…

'And I suppose I was hoping she would listen to me for once…'

Nell didn't even grace that with the spitting answer sitting on her tongue. Turning, she began striding down the hillside, leaving Xander cursing colourfully as he gathered up their scattered things.

She knew that mother and son did not enjoy a warm relationship, in fact the best she could describe it as was cool. They met, they embraced, they threw veiled but heavily barbed comments at each other; they embraced then parted again until the next time. It was like standing in the middle of a minefield when they were together. One step out of line and Nell had a feeling that they would both ignite and explode all over her, so she'd tended to keep very quiet and still in their company.

Not that it happened often. It wasn't as if with a relationship like that mother and son lived in each other's pockets. Xander had his life and Gabriela had hers—par for the course with Xander's relationships, she tagged on acidly. The very few times that Nell had come into contact with both of them together was usually at one of those formal functions Xander would drag her to occasionally—to keep up appearances while Vanessa hovered around somewhere in the murky background, awaiting her lover's return.

Her skin turned cold as she thought that.

A shriek of delight suddenly filled the hillside, dragging her attention down the hill towards the house. She saw that the helicopter had settled next to the other one and Gabriela was now standing by the pool with her arms thrown wide open while Thea Sophia hurried towards her clapping her hands with delight.

To witness the dauntingly sophisticated Gabriela dressed in immaculate lavender silk fold the little black-clad bundle that was Thea Sophia to her in a noisily loving hug came as almost as big a surprise as the way Nell had just behaved with Xander up on the hill.

Where had all the warmth and affection come from? She would never have believed Gabriela capable of it if she was not seeing it with her own eyes.

The two faces of the Pascalis family, she thought grimly as she maintained a brisk pace downwards. Behind her was a man who had been as cold as ice for ninety-nine per cent of their marriage, suddenly showing her he had passion hot enough to singe layers from her skin! Now here was the drop-dead sophisticated mother putting on a demonstration of childlike adoration that would shock her peers—though anyone would love Thea Sophia, she then had to add with a brief softening inside. The sweet old lady would make the devil want to give her a loving hug.

As the two embracing women dropped out of sight behind the red-tiled roof of the house, Nell felt the silly burn of tears sting her eyes. It was stupid to feel hurt by such an open display of affection from Xander's mother for his aunt, but that was exactly what she did feel. Gabriela had never greeted her like that, never welcomed her with open arms and shrieks of delight. On those few tension-charged occasions they had met just the brief air-kissing of Gabriela's perfumed cheeks had always made Nell feel as if she were desecrating holy ground.

Or was it the other way around and she was the one who repelled deeper displays of affection? Had those defensive shells Xander talked about kept her mother-in-law at arm's length? She didn't know. She didn't even know if Gabriela knew the full truth about the true disaster that her son's marriage was.

The two women had gone from the pool area by the time Nell reached it. Making directly for the rinse shower that occupied a corner of the patio area, she switched it on and began washing the dust from her feet. The bottom of her foot still stung from its contact with the sharp stone, but as she was about to lift up the foot to inspect it she saw Xander arrive a few paces behind her and her full attention became fixed on him.

He had gathered up their things and was now placing them on one of the tables, tall, dark, uncomfortably alluring with his shiny wet hair, loose clothes and bare feet. Nothing like the man she was used to seeing—nothing. The other Xander was all skin-tingling, sophisticated charisma; this one was all—sex.

She looked away as he turned towards her, stiffened like mad when his hands snaked around her waist to gently crush fine muslin against her skin. A long brown foot with long brown toes appeared next to her foot so he could share the water sprinkling down on them.

Next the smoothness of his cheek arrived against her cheek. 'We are being watched, *agapita*,' he warned huskily as she tried to pull away from him.

It was all he needed to say to halt her attempt to escape. So she clamped her teeth together, kept her chin lowered and swapped one cleaned foot for the other and felt the intimacy deep in her trembling bones in watching Xander do the same thing.

'You're trembling all over. I like it,' he remarked in a sexy, husky groan by her ear, felt the heat mount her cheek and laughed softly as he brushed his lips against that tell-tale heat.

'I'm trembling because I'm angry with you,' she said. 'Look at me, Xander,' she then said heavily. 'I'm all wet and salty and now I have to go in there and meet your mother looking like this. You should have given me more warning then at least I could have found time to shower and change before she arrived…and she will know, won't she,' she then added unhappily, 'what the papers have been saying about us?'

'And that bothers you.'

'It bothers you too or you would not have brought me here and hidden me away like you have.'

His foot disappeared and she sensed a new grimness in him as he reached over her shoulder to turn off the shower. 'I did not bring you here to hide you,' he denied.

'Yes, you did. The same as you've been hiding me away all year.'

'So you thought you would make me wake up and take notice by involving yourself with another man?'

'Isn't that just typically arrogant of you to think I was trying to grab your attention?' She tried to move away again but he still would not allow it, the flat of his hand resting lightly but firmly against her stomach to keep her trapped in front of him. She sucked in a short, tense breath. 'I was leaving you, Xander,' she stated bluntly. 'And I was going, hoping never to set eyes on you again.'

'You did more than set eyes on me a few minutes ago, Nell, and I don't recall you turning away. In fact…' He turned her to face him. His eyes wore a hard glitter. 'I would say that you could not get enough of what you saw.'

'That was just sex.'

'And you know so much about it to sound so dismissive?'

Nell didn't answer. She was glaring at the ribbon of hard brown skin dressed with crisp dark hair showing between his gaping shirt and wishing with all her heart that her tongue didn't tingle with a desire to taste.

'We were talking about your mother.' She slewed her eyes sideways to stare at the glinting pool.

'She's here to discuss some family business.'

'Well, maybe she will be kind enough to give me a lift off this island when she leaves.'

'You think I would allow it?'

Green eyes flashed into contact with his. 'Would you like to repeat that bit about not hiding me?'

He went several steps further and lowered his dark head and kissed her, not hot and driven like before but slow and gentle with just enough passion to elicit a response. 'That is why you're here, *agape mou*,' he murmured as he lifted his head again. 'We are going to kick-start this marriage. *Then* let us see if you still wish to leave.'

Xander could say this in *that* tone of voice because she'd responded. He could say it because her fingers were already in contact with his brown skin. This beautiful, defiant, contrary creature might not want to want him but hell, she did want him, Xander thought grimly.

Letting go of her, he strode off, leaving her standing there knowing that he had won that little battle without her putting up much of a defence.

Waiting in the coolness of the foyer, he viewed Nell's arrival in the open doorway through carefully hooded eyes and had to lock his jaw to keep other parts of him under control. Lit from behind by the sunlight, she looked like a sea nymph standing in the jaws of a hungry shark.

He was the hungry shark. If they had been alone here he would be closing those jaws and carrying her off to finish what he'd started out there. He'd laid down the gauntlet as to where this marriage of theirs was going to go from here and by the way she was hovering in the doorway he would say that she knew she did not stand a chance of changing that course.

She began walking forward. As he watched her come closer his head played a tempting little scene that involved him carrying her up the stairs and laying her on the bed then stripping away the few scraps she wore.

Though maybe he would leave the G-string in place, he thought darkly, seeing his mouth tracing its skimpy white lines with a chain of tongue-tipped kisses that would have her begging him to take it off.

That was how he wanted her—begging. He wanted her spreading those slender golden thighs and inviting him in. He wanted her arms around his neck and her eyes pleading and—

A frown clipped his brows together. 'Go and make yourself presentable while I entertain our—guest,' he instructed.

'But your mother will think it rude if I don't—'

His eyes made a glinting sweep over the now damp strip of Indian cotton that was doing so little to hide the brevity of what was beneath. 'Trust me, you will feel better if you take time to change.'

A self-conscious flush mounted her cheeks. 'You don't look so presentable yourself,' she still had the spirit to hit back as she walked by him.

Xander just grinned. 'The difference being that I don't care what other people think when they look at me.'

Only because he still managed to look fabulous even with bare feet and his damp shirt lying open down his hair-tangled, muscle-contoured, bronzed front, Nell thought as she took to the stairs without further argument.

If she'd looked back she would have caught him quickly fastening buttons and combing long fingers through his hair. And the expression on his face had changed from lazily indifferent to grim.

He could have done without this intrusion from his mother today of all days. When she had rung his apartment in Athens this morning with an urgent request to see him, only to be told he was coming to the island, the last thing he had expected was for her to promptly invite herself and he'd told her not to come.

Though in truth, now she was here, he had some things of his own he needed to thrash out with his mother, things he preferred to get out of the way before his single-minded seduction of his beautiful wife continued along its present course.

Thinking about that exciting creature he'd met in the cove an hour ago set his nerves on edge. Nell had turned the tables on him with her provocative performance, and what was bothering him was why she had done it.

As the aggravating witch had just pointed out, three weeks ago she had been leaving him for another man.

A man, no less, that she'd been trying to contact via the telephone in his study here ever since she'd arrived on the island, but, like himself and the small army of people he had out there looking for him, Nell had discovered that Marcel Dubois had effectively disappeared from the face of the earth.

Scared of the repercussions when he heard of Nell's accident and knew that her husband was about to find out about them? If so, the Frenchman should have thought about those repercussions sooner—before he lured Nell into taking flight.

But that was not the point that was troubling Xander right now as he stood outside the salon door, grimly tidying himself. Nell was still trying to contact the cowardly swine yet she'd responded to him like a woman who'd been suppressing her desires for too long.

Hedging her bets? Using him as a substitute for her new love? Had that bastard woken her up to her own sexual desires and after three weeks without him she was hungry enough to let any man have her—even the one she believed was having an affair with another woman?

Anger bit its sharp teeth into him at the mere idea of another man taking what belonged to him. He threw open the salon door and stepped inside to the smell of his mother's perfume and to see an aunt who was all beaming smiles because her favourite person had come for a visit.

Shame that the son did not feel the same way. 'OK, Madre, let us make this brief. I have more important things to do than listen to your business troubles today.'

'I think you have already been dealing with your—business, caro,' his mother drawled with a swift up-and-down glance of his dishevelled state despite the attempt to tidy up. 'And there was I, thinking as I flew here that at last Alexander will know what it feels like when a marriage flounders on the rocks...'

'Your marriage did not flounder; you scuppered it,' he incised.

'If you two are going to fight I will leave you,' Thea Sophia put in and headed for the door, her beaming smile lost. 'You might also like to embrace each other *before* you tear each other to pieces,' she added sternly before she walked out.

Fifteen minutes later and Nell was coming down the stairs again after the quickest shower on record and with her freshly washed hair rough-dried by an urgent towel then left to do its own thing while she scrambled around for something suitable to wear. The fact that whoever had packed for her in England had chosen almost all of the clothes she'd bought for her non-existent honeymoon did not make the choice a simple one. One, the clothes had been bought with Xander and romance in mind. Two, they were now a full season out of date. So to have to put on one of the slinky off-the-shoulder short dresses in last season's rich jade colour did not give her confidence a major boost as she hovered outside the salon door, running nervous fingers down a mid-thigh-length dress that might do good things for her eyes and her figure but was going to look out-of-date to her super-elegant, fashion-guru mother-in-law.

That she'd stepped into a war zone took Nell about two seconds to register. Xander was lounging in one of the chairs, looking for the world like the king of all he surveyed even with bare feet—while he shot angry sparks at his mother.

Gabriela was sitting opposite him, giving the cool appearance that she did not notice the sparks. Heaven had left nothing out when they made this beautiful woman, Nell thought enviously. The sleek black hair, the sensational dark eyes, the long, slender figure which could pull off any fashion statement with panache.

As he turned his head to look at her, Nell felt a blush coming on as Xander let his eyes narrow then linger on her shining hair with its still damp, spiralling ends touching the hollow of her back. She'd tugged the dress up onto her shoulders as far as it would let her but it still looked low-cut at the front and slinky—as those too expressive eyes had already assessed.

'Ah, Helen, there you are.' Her mother-in-law's smooth voice brought her eyes swinging in her direction as Gabriela rose gracefully to her feet. 'You look delightful, *cara*,' she smiled as she came towards her, her expression revealing nothing as she swung her eyes down over Nell's dress, but the criticism was there, Nell was sure that it was. 'Enchantingly clean and fresh as you always look,' Gabriela added, then they air-kissed while Nell tried not to cringe at the 'clean and fresh' bit. 'And such hair! I am sure it grows two inches longer each time I see you. You know,' she eyed Nell shrewdly, 'with the touch of a gifted stylist I know in Milan it could be the most—'

'You will leave Nell's hair alone,' Gabriela's son interrupted as he rose to his feet. 'I like it exactly the way it is.'

'Don't be snappy, *caro*,' his mother scolded. 'I was only going to suggest that if you gave me a week with Helen in Milan I could truly turn her into—'

'I will extend on that,' Xander put in. 'You will leave Nell alone altogether. I like *all* of her exactly the way that she is.'

'Well, of course you do,' his mother agreed. 'But—'

'*Exquisito, mi amore.*' Placing his mouth to Nell's cheek, Xander spoke right over whatever Gabriela's but was going to be. 'Don't listen to her,' he advised. 'I do not need another fashion slave in this family.'

'I am not a slave to fashion!' his mother protested.

'The couture houses of Europe wipe their feet on you, Madre, and you know what makes it so crazy?' He looked down on her from his superior height. 'You would look amazing in whatever you chose to wear, be it sackcloth. They should be paying you to wear their clothes.'

'They do,' Gabriela informed him stiffly. Then because, like Nell, Gabriela clearly did not know if he was teasing or being cruel, 'Oh, go away and put some dry clothes on,' she snapped, wafting a slender white hand at him. 'You make a compliment sound like an insult and confuse me.'

Xander made no attempt to enlighten her as to which had

been his intention. He was angry, Nell noticed, so she had to assume the insult was what he'd meant.

He went obediently enough though, pausing long enough to assure Nell that he would be back before Thea Sophia arrived with refreshment for them all. The door closing behind him left Nell and Gabriela alone with a small silence to fill.

Gabriela did it. 'We were arguing when you came in, as I am sure you noticed. Alexander likes to have things all his own way but cannot always have it.'

The way her eyes slid away from Nell made her wonder if the argument had been about her.

Or the ugly rumours about their marriage seemed likely.

'Strong men are like that,' Nell found herself saying—as if she knew much about them.

'You think him strong?' Gabriela quizzed thoughtfully. 'I think him arrogant to believe that I should sacrifice my... Ah, but let us not talk about it.' She cut herself off from saying what she had been about to say right at the intriguing point, as far as Nell was concerned. 'Tell me about your accident and how you are recovering,' she invited. 'A much more interesting subject...'

By the time they'd done to death the scant details Nell was prepared to give about her accident and her ensuing recovery, which she suspected by the far-away expression Gabriela barely heard, Thea Sophia arrived and the odd mood lightened as Gabriela found a true smile as she went to take the heavy tray from the older woman.

There was a small tussle, which Thea won, as Nell knew from experience that she would.

'Leave me be, Gabriela,' she said. 'I must feel useful or I may as well take to my bed and wait for God to come and get me.'

'Wait for God indeed,' Gabriela mocked as she went to sit down and the older woman crossed the room to set down the tray. 'What you need, Thea, is to be taken out of yourself. When was the last time you left this brown dot of an island?'

'This brown dot is Pascalis land,' the old lady responded. 'And you might not have liked it here, but I love it.'

'Which did not answer my question.'

'I do not recall when I last left it.'

'Then it is high time that you did. Since Alexander refuses to let me make-over his wife, I think I will take you to Milan, Thea, and we will give you a complete make-over then find you a passionate man who will stop you talking about waiting for God.'

To Nell's surprise the old lady let out an amused chuckle. 'He will be too old to fulfil my hidden passions.'

'Not these days, *carisima*,' Xander's mother came back. 'Today the old men have the Viagra to maintain their flagging passions and will be very useful indeed to you. No, don't sit down right over there, Helen. Come and sit here beside me.'

'Wicked creature.' Sophia spoke over Gabriela's command while Nell meekly did as she had been told. 'If my nephew were still alive he would lock you in your room for speaking so disrespectfully to me.'

'Ah, four years and I still miss Demitri,' Gabriela sighed wistfully.

'I was twenty-three when the war took my Gregoris and made me a widow but I still miss him every single day.'

It was news to Nell that Thea Sophia had been married!

'You miss his *passions*, Sophia?' Gabriela prodded teasingly.

'Of course!' the old lady declared. 'He was a big, strong, handsome man—as with all the Pascalis men. My bed felt cold for years.'

'I understand the feeling,' Gabriela sighed. 'Maybe we should go to Milan to find ourselves a new man each. A cold bed is no pleasure, Thea. You would have liked my husband, *cara*.' She turned to include Nell in the conversation. 'Alexander is just like him—hewn from rock on the outside and deliciously protective by nature, but so jealously possessive of me that he rarely let me out of his sight. Yet what did he do but go and die in two short seconds while I was out of the room!'

'What is this—a wake?' Xander strode in on the conversation, wearing pale chinos and a fresh white shirt.

'Your father was my one abiding love,' his mother said sadly.

'Maybe he was, but you…'

The rest of the 'but' was completed in some cutting Italian that literally froze the discussion and turned Gabriela pale.

Thea Sophia recovered first, bursting into a flurry of chatter as she handed out the small cups of strong black Greek coffee and Nell puzzled over what Xander could he have said this time to destroy his mother as effectively as that.

She cast him a hateful look, which he returned with a grimace that seemed to say he was already regretting whatever he'd said. But no apology was offered and after giving him as long as it took him to lower himself into the chair he had been occupying earlier, Nell flicked him another hard look then turned to Gabriela.

'A trip to Milan sounds very exciting,' she said. 'I've never been there and I've had a yen to have my hair cut—short and spiky,' she added for good measure while Gabriela's eyes began to glow. She knew what Nell was doing and it was working. Xander shifted in his chair. 'Perhaps I could come with you,' she suggested. 'It would be fun to spend lots of money on new clothes and things, try out a new image—'

'Try for a full recovery before you make any plans,' Xander grimly put in.

'I am recovered,' Nell insisted. He was eyeing her narrowly, warning sparks glinting at her now instead of his mother. 'I've had two whole weeks under Thea Sophia's tender care to aid my recovery.'

'You were the good patient,' Sophia put in, bending to pat Nell's cheek fondly as she handed her a cup of coffee. 'You should have seen the extent of her bruising, Gabriela,' she declared in dismay. 'No wonder Alexander could not bear to look at them. Where were his protective instincts when this poor girl drove her flimsy car into a tree? She was bruised from here to here.' A gnarled hand drew a slashing left-to-right diagonal line in the air across Nell's chest then added the other line across her stomach.

Nell saw Xander's brows shift into a sharp frown as he watched the vivid demonstration take place.

'Car seat-belt burns, Helen called them,' his aunt continued in disgust. 'I call them criminal. Who would want to ever wear a seat belt again if they had suffered such damage?'

'Think of the damage without the belt, Thea,' her great-nephew pointed out. 'Nell lost her appendix, cracked her ribs and got off lightly into the bargain, if you want the truth.'

'While you were on the other side of the world getting your name in the newspapers and—'

'That is enough, Sophia…'

It was Gabriela's quiet command that brought a halt to it, her dark eyes flickering from Nell's suddenly pale face to her son's cold, closed one. The old lady resorted to mumbled Greek as she bustled back to her coffee tray, leaving a tense silence in her wake.

It screeched in Nell's head like chalk across a blackboard— a white chalk that had scraped itself across her cheeks. She wanted to jump up and run out of the room but she didn't think her trembling limbs would make it. So she stared down at the brimming cup of strong black coffee she balanced on its saucer and tried to swallow the lump of humiliation that was blocking her throat.

She'd known that her useless marriage was public property so why should she feel so upset that Thea Sophia was so willing to remark on it?

Xander shifted in his chair and she flinched a look at him from beneath her eyelashes. His eyes were fixed on her, narrowed and intense.

The lump in her throat changed into a burn as tears decided to take its place. In desperation she turned to Gabriela.

'How—how long do you plan on staying?' she asked in a polite voice that came out too husky.

Her mother-in-law was looking at her in dark sympathy, which hurt almost as much as Thea's thoughtless words had done. As Gabriela opened her mouth to answer, Xander got there before her.

'She will not be staying.' It was blunt to the point of rude.

Nell ignored him. 'It w-would be nice if you could stay a few days,' she invited. 'W-we could get to know each other better—'

'My mother does not do getting-to-know-you, *agape mou*,' Xander's hateful voice intruded yet again. 'She lives a much too rarefied life, hmm, Madre?'

Gabriela's lips snapped together then opened again. Like Nell, she was grimly ignoring her sarcastic son. 'I am afraid I cannot stay,' she murmured apologetically. 'I came because I need to discuss some business with my son.'

'Just business?' he mocked.

Nell couldn't take any more, ridding herself of the coffee-cup, she jumped to her feet. 'What is it with you?' she flashed at the sarcastic devil. 'Trying to have a polite conversation with you around is like living inside a tabloid newspaper—full of sarcasm and innuendo!'

'That just about covers it,' Xander agreed.

'Oh, why don't you just shut up?' she cried, making Thea Sophia jerk to attention, and Gabriela's eyes opened wide. 'You know what your problem is, Xander? You are still that resentful little boy who swam alone in the sea. You forgot to grow up!'

'*I* forgot to grow up?' Xander climbed to his feet. 'Where the hell have you been for the last year?'

'Right where you put me until I decided I'd had enough of it,' Nell answered fiercely. Cheeks hot now, green eyes alight with rage.

'So you decided it would be fun to drive you car into a tree?'

Fun? He thought she had done it for *fun*? 'Well, we all know what you were doing because you featured in the newspapers so prominently,' she tossed back. 'Would you like me to tell them what I was doing while I was having *fun* crashing my car?'

'Watch it, Nell.'

Now he was deadly serious. You could cut the tension with a knife. Nell's chin shot up. Xander towered over her by several intimidating inches but she faced up to his threatening stance.

Shall I tell them? her angry eyes challenged him while their audience sat riveted and the desire to unlock her aching throat and shatter his impossible pride to smithereens set the blood pounding in her head.

His face did not move, not even by an eyelash, hard, handsome and utterly unyielding like a perfectly sculptured mask. The cold eyes, the flat lips, the flaring nostrils—he was warning her not to do it—*daring* her to do it.

The pounding changed to a violent tingling. Taking Xander on was becoming a drug that sang like a craving she just had to feed. Her lips parted, quivering, and that stone-like expression still did not alter even though he knew it was coming—he *knew*!

Then another voice dropped cool, calm, curiously into the thrumming tension, 'Helen, darling, did you know you are bleeding from the base of your foot...?'

CHAPTER SIX

NELL broke vital eye contact with Xander to glance dazedly down at her foot, where, sure enough, blood was oozing onto the base of her strappy mule. The sharp stone on the hillside, she remembered, and was about to explain when Xander struck, seizing the opportunity to scoop her up off the ground!

'Get off me, you great brute!' she shot out in surprised anger.

'Shut up!' he hissed as he carried her from the room.

'I have never seen such fire,' Thea Sophia gasped into the stunned space they left in the tension behind them. 'The child has been as quiet and as sweet as a mountain stream all the time she has been here.'

'She's certainly found her voice now,' Gabriela drily responded.

'She's found more than her voice,' Xander bit down at her as the salon door swung shut behind them and he strode across the foyer, heading straight for the stairs. 'She's found a compelling desire for a death wish!'

'Not feeling so sarcastic now?' Nell hit right back, still fizzing and popping inside with fury.

He stopped on the stairs, blazing black eyes capturing sparking green. His wide, sensual mouth was tight with fury, nostrils flaring like warning flags. The cold mask had broken, she saw, and felt the hectic sting of a dangerous excitement vibrate just about every skin pore.

'You are goading me for some reason,' he ripped down at her. 'I want to know why!'

'Death wish?' Nell answered in defiance, only to bury her top teeth in her bottom lip when his glittering eyes narrowed for a moment, widened—then flared.

He caught that bottom lip with his own teeth and robbed it

79

from her. As she drew in a startled gasp he held on and sucked, turning the whole crazy thing into a very erotic kiss.

Downstairs in the salon Thea Sophia made a jerky move to follow them. 'They will need—'

'Stay where you are, Thea,' Gabriela murmured quietly. 'I don't think they will appreciate the intrusion right now.'

'Oh.' Thea stopped.

'Mmm,' Gabriela agreed with the older woman's dawning expression. 'Your calm mountain spring is about to turn into a raging torrent, *cara*,' she said thoughtfully. 'And our angry, high-principled boy is about to learn what it is like to be caught up in such an uncontrolled flood.'

'You sound pleased about that.'

'Pleased?' Gabriela considered. 'I suppose I am. He never forgave me my raging torrent. Let him learn and understand how I felt.'

'Those two are man and wife. Your torrent took place out of wedlock and devastated more people than you care to recall,' Thea said curtly.

The sighed-out 'Yes,' took place as Gabriela came to her feet then walked restlessly over to the window, where she stood staring out at the glinting swimming pool, beyond which lay a crescent beach and an ocean of glistening blue.

'I've had enough of this place,' she decided suddenly and, turning back to the room, went to collect her purse. 'Tell Alexander we will deal with our business some other time—'

'Oh, I did not mean to chase you away, Gabriela,' Sophia said anxiously.

'I know.' Gabriela kissed the old woman's worried cheek. 'But I should not have come. Alexander did warn me he had no time for my problems and now I know why.'

'They've been apart for two weeks, Gabriela.'

'They've been apart for much longer than that, Thea.' Gabriela smiled ruefully at the older woman's rose-tinted view of life. 'Those two might be married, my sweet darling,' she broke the news gently, 'but they are not yet man and wife...'

The kiss lasted all the way up the stairs and into the bedroom. Nell only thought to pull back from it when she heard the door slam behind them with the help of a foot. Xander watched the liquid bewilderment darken her beautiful eyes as she stared up at him. He could feel her heart racing beneath the flat of his palm.

'I'm going to ravish you senseless until you tell me what it is you are up to,' he bit out thinly.

The heart rate speeded up. 'I'm not up to anything!' she denied.

But her cheeks began to heat—a sure sign that she was lying, the little witch. 'You have been playing me hot and cold since I arrived here! Do you think I cannot tell when someone has a hidden agenda? And don't blink those innocent eyes at me,' he rasped. 'I know when my strings are being pulled!'

'*Your* strings are being pulled?' Nell tried to wriggle free of his arms but he was having none of it, strong muscles flexed in a show of pure male strength. 'You've been threatening to ravish me since you turned up at my sick-bed!'

'What a good idea,' he gritted out with a teeth-clenching smile and headed for the bed.

Oh, my God, Nell thought and started to tremble. 'My foot!' she jerked out in the wild hope it would pull him up short.

It did. He stopped in the middle of the bedroom, cleft chin flexing, tiny explosions of angry frustration taking place in his eyes. Without a word he changed direction, carrying her into the bathroom, where he slotted her down on the marble top between the his-and-hers washbasins.

Her hair stroked Xander's face as she straightened away from him, her fingers trailing a reluctant withdrawal from around his neck. Her heart was still racing, the fine tremors attacking her slender frame, making his teeth grit together because he couldn't decide if they were tremors of anger or desire.

It was novel; he didn't think he'd ever been in this kind of situation before in which he was having to out-guess the confusing signals he was being sent. Women usually fell on him— wholesale. Having this beautiful, contrary creature try her best to tie him in knots was stinging to life senses he'd had no idea he possessed.

A taste for the fight. A deeply grudging willingness to play the game for a while just to see where she thought she was going with it. He knew where it was going. Hell, he was already there. She might have earned herself some respite with the injured foot but that was all it was—a brief time-out while the rest of it throbbed and pulsed in the quickened heat of his blood.

Reaching above her head, he opened a cupboard and fished around for a clean cloth and some other bits and pieces he kept up there. He was standing between her legs, her thighs touching his thighs and she wasn't moving a muscle. Yet another surge dragged on his senses as he dropped his arms and saw the way she was staring at the flexing muscles beneath his shirt. Narrowing his eyes, he watched as the tip of her tongue sneaked out to moisten her upper lip as he ran his fingers lightly down her thighs to go in search of the offending foot.

Mine, he thought as he watched that nervy pink tongue-tip, and let his hands pause so his fingers could draw some light, experimental circles across the soft skin behind her knees. She jolted as if he'd shot her. Her chin came up, their eyes clashed, his carefully unfathomable, hers as dark and disturbed as hell.

'Foot,' he said.

Her teeth replaced the tongue-tip, burying into the full bottom lip as she lifted her knee so he could grasp her ankle and remove her shoe. One glance down and he realised she'd offered him the wrong foot.

'The left not the right,' he said then began to frown. Something was niggling him about the left and the right side of this aggravating woman. What could aggravate him when they both looked more or less the same?

Beautiful, perfect, ripe for seduction.

She offered him the other foot. Removing the shoe, he dipped his head and used the cloth to wipe away the blood so he could check out the cut.

'You did this on the hill,' he recalled and she nodded.

'It didn't bleed then. The hot shower I took must have aggravated it—ouch,' she added when he pressed the pad of her foot around the small cut in search of foreign bodies.

Her toes wriggled, small, pink, slender toes with a shading of gold across their tops from the sun.

Xander's tongue moistened. 'Feel anything in there?'

'No. It's just stinging a bit.'

'Clean cuts do.'

'Speaks the voice of experience,' she mocked huskily.

Swapping the cloth for a packet of antiseptic pads, he ripped a sachet open with his teeth.

'I wet-shave,' he answered, bringing those incredible eyes flickering curiously up to stare at his lean, smooth chin. That pink tip of a tongue returned to replace the teeth as she studied him with a fascination that set the skin all over his body tingling. If this wasn't the most intimate she'd ever been with a man—not counting the interlude in the cove—then he did not know women as he thought he did.

'I cut myself sometimes. Usually when I'm—distracted.'

The colour bloomed in her cheeks as she caught his meaning. 'Hence the antiseptic pads.' She sounded breathless.

'And wound strips.' He ripped the protective cover off a small plaster next and bent to press it over the cleaned cut.

But he didn't let go, his gaze recapturing hers as his thumb began lightly stoking the smooth, padded flesh at the base of her foot in the same circling action he had used on the backs of her knees. Silence followed. He didn't think she was even breathing. No two people had ever been more aware as to where this was leading and any second now she was going to disappear in a shower of her own prickling static.

'Xander...' His name feathered helplessly from her.

He responded by releasing the foot so he could run his hands back up the length of her legs—only this time he slid them beneath the clingy little dress.

'You are gorgeous, you know that?' he murmured softly.

'You don't have to say—'

'Gorgeous eyes, gorgeous hair, smooth, satin skin...' His

hands moved higher in a slow, sensual glide. 'You have the heart-shaped face of an angel and the mouth of a siren, the blush of a virgin and the teasing skills of a whore.'

'That isn't—'

With a controlled tug he slid her towards him across cold marble until she fitted neatly to his front. Her eyes widened when she felt the hardening thickness at his crotch. He felt her revealing little quiver, watched her breasts shift on a stifled little gasp. Then her thighs tightened against him, narrowing his eyes on her very—very expressive face.

'You like this, don't you?' he taunted lazily.

Nell dragged her eyes away. 'I don't know what you're talking about.'

'Sex, *agape mou*,' he named it. 'You are quivering with delight because you love to know you can affect me like this.'

'For all I know you're like this with any woman you come into contact with,' she tossed at him, making a jerky shift in an effort to move back.

His hands held her clamped to him. His hips gave a slow, smooth, sensual thrust. She quivered like a trapped little bird as damp heat spread across the exposed and vulnerable centre of her sex.

'Do I apply the same reasoning to your response?'

He knew what was happening to her, Nell realised. How could he not when she was so burning hot? A stifled gasp shot from her when he bent his head, his lips moulding hers and taking control of them, his tongue darting into her mouth. Each time they did this it got worse, she thought dizzily as she fell into it with a hopeless groan and let her slender arms snake up and around his neck.

She felt strong muscles flex in his shoulders as he lifted her up from the marble, felt the hard and pulsing sexual promise in his body as he flattened her to his chest. Her legs had wrapped themselves tightly around him and they might as well have been back in the ocean with no clothes on because she could feel everything that was happening to him.

It was only when he tipped her down onto the bed that she

realised where they were now. With a gasping drag on her unwilling lips she broke the kiss to look around her. With a swimming sense of disorientation noticed for the first time that since she'd taken her shower earlier someone had been in here and closed the shutters over the windows to keep out the fierce heat of the afternoon sun. The room had a warm, soft, sultry feel to it as if it had been deliberately set for making love.

Even the bedcovers had been drawn back, she realised. Her gaze flicked back to the man lying in a languid stretch beside her on the bed, lazily reading each expression as it passed across her face. He offered her a mocking smile. The air went perfectly still in her lungs. He'd done it. When he'd come up to take his own shower he'd come in here and made this room ready for seduction as if it had always been a forgone conclusion that it was going to happen this afternoon.

'No,' she pushed out across taut throat muscles.

He merely held on to the smile and brushed a stray lock of Titian silk from her suddenly pale cheek. 'I've spent a whole year imagining you lying here with your beautiful hair splayed out around you and your beautiful mouth warmed and pulsing as it awaits the pleasure of mine.'

Sensation trickled right down the front of her. 'We are not going to do this,' she insisted shakily.

For an answer he began to unbutton his shirt. Nell stared as warm, bronzed skin roughened by dark hair began to make its appearance. Everything about him said man on a course he would not be moved from. Real alarm struck her with a frightening clarity.

She drew in a taut breath. 'Y-your m-mother,' she reminded him. 'W-we—'

'I don't need her permission to do this, *agape mou*,' he drawled.

'But she—'

He moved, long fingers leaving the shirt to come and frame her heart-shaped face from pale cheek to trembling chin. Pinpricks leapt across the surface of her skin as he bent to brush his mouth across hers. 'No more reprieves,' he murmured very softy. 'This is it, my beautiful Helen. It is time to face your fate because it is here…'

Her fate. Nell stared at him. He was deadly serious. To her horror he began to stroke the hand down her throat and across her shoulder, fingertips pushing stretchy jade fabric out of his way.

'Stop it!' she choked out and at last found the sense to put up a fight.

Dark eyes lit with a kind of cold amusement that chilled her as he captured her flailing fists and flattened them to the bed above her head. 'The little game you've been playing with me is over,' he said grimly. 'Accept it, for you are about to get your just desserts.'

'You're angry,' she gasped in shocked realisation.

His tight grimace confirmed it.

'But—why?'

The innocent question locked his lean, handsome face. 'I've done nothing but treat you with respect since we married and you paid me back by leaving me for another man.'

With his free hand he went back to undoing shirt buttons in a grim display of intent.

'Just thank your lucky stars that you did not make it, my beautiful Helen,' he glinted down at her. 'Or you would not be about to enjoy Alexander Pascalis the lover, but the other Alexander Pascalis—the one that makes big men quake in fear!'

'How do you know I didn't make it?' she prodded recklessly, staring as more and more of that muscled, bronzed, hair-roughened chest appeared. 'How do you know I didn't *make it* a dozen times during the week Hugo Vance wasn't around to stop it from happening?' she choked up at him. '*Before* I decided to leave you for good!'

The fingers stopped working the buttons. Nell heaved in a wary breath of air as a *frisson* of alarm shot across her heaving breasts.

'But you didn't, did you?'

It was a very seriously driven warning to be careful what

she said next, making her wish her mouth would just shut up—
but it wouldn't. He might already be wearing the face that made
big men quake, but she had a whole year's-worth of unfairness
pounding away inside her, and it needed to be heard.

'Y-you left me alone on our wedding night,' she reminded
him, beginning to struggle again to get free. He subdued her
by clamping a leg across her thighs. 'You refused to make
excuses or defend yourself—you couldn't even be bothered to
lie! I've had to live with that, Xander, not you. Y-you just went
back to your life and didn't care what you left behind!' Tears
were threatening, making her soft mouth quiver and turning
her eyes into deep green pools of hurt. 'W-well, you left me
behind w-with a twenty-four-hour guard to do the caring for
you! If I went to the local village shop Hugo Vance came along
with me. He had to do—he was in charge of the remote control
for the wretched gates!'

'He was there for your safety,' he bit back impatiently.

'He was there to control your limp rag of a wife!' she cried.
'You said that you and I are alike; w-well, tell me, Xander,
would you have lived my life for the last year without doing
something about it?'

'But I repeat—you didn't, did you, Nell?'

Nell lay there beneath him heaving and panting, his leg
heavy across her legs and her shining hair caught beneath the
hands he still pinned above her head. She glared hotly into a
face that was coldly mask-like, reminding her of that rock his
mother had talked about. And the stinging pinpricks attacking
her flesh were the sparks of her mutiny bouncing right off him.

Hewn, hard, handsome and so threatening she shivered. Yet
backing down now just wasn't an option she was prepared to
take. 'Do you think you are the only one that can be discreet
about their lovers?' she heard herself dare to challenge. 'Do
you think that because you didn't want me I should think myself unfit for anyone else?'

Maybe she did have a death wish, she thought tensely as a
new level of stillness locked his hard eyes on her face with an
expression that was too frighteningly inexplicable to dare to

read. He was eleven years older than Nell and at that precise moment she felt every one of those years boring holes into her head.

'Are you telling me—without the guts to make the full statement,' he pushed out finally, 'that you have taken lovers since you married me?'

Nell's quivering upper lip had to fight to break free from her bottom lip. 'Would it make me a lesser person in your eyes if I said yes?' she quavered huskily. 'Perhaps totally unfit for you to touch?'

It was living on the edge, Nell knew that as she said it, feeling more afraid of what she was prodding here than she dared let herself think. But she needed to know. She'd lived the last year loving a man who'd locked her up in a glass bubble marked, 'Virgin. Sole possession of Alexander Pascalis', as if it was the only thing about her that made her worthy of the place she held in his life, while he blithely continued to bed his mistress as if that was perfectly OK.

But the real point she was making was, would he still want to be here with her without the provenance?

A stifled gasp escaped when his hand came to rest beneath her breast, where her heart was racing madly. It began a gentle stroking as he lay stretched out, half beside her, half on top of her, a look of grim contemplation taking charge of his face. She'd stop fighting to get free and had never felt more vulnerable because she just didn't know what he was going to say or do next. His eyes weren't telling her, his expression wasn't telling her, even the light stroke of this hand wasn't telling her anything because she wasn't sure that he was aware it was doing it.

It was a test, Xander knew that. He was not so blinded by those beautiful flashing eyes and this sensational body he had pinned to the bed that he could not recognise a challenge when it was being tossed at him.

What he could not decipher was if the reckless little witch was talking like this because she wanted to hit him hard with the truth or because she was taunting him with the possibility of it being the truth.

Was it the truth?

He still did not know. She had still not made that *yes* a full-blown, bloody statement of fact.

Did it make a difference to how he felt?

To wanting to make love to her? Not the slightest difference to the desire pounding away in his blood.

To this creature he had respected more than anyone else in his entire life? Hell, yes, it made a difference there. Nell belonged to him. She wore his ring on her slender white finger. She had loved him so much once that he refused to believe that she was capable of making love with any other man but him.

But he discovered he was scared that in a fit of rebellion she might have done.

He pulled in a deep breath. The atmosphere was so thick with his long silence that he could taste it on his tongue as he slid his hand up to cover her breast. Its receptive tip stung to life to push into his palm and another strangled gasp escaped her soft, quivering mouth.

He looked at her hair spread out across the cover like a burnished copper halo. Then at her face, heart-shaped, exquisite but wary as hell. His eyelashes glossed over his gaze, dipped lower, across the smooth-as-silk shoulder he had exposed that looked so sexy and inviting, then further to where his long fingers cupped her breast over sensually moulding jade-coloured fabric. The tips of his fingers were in tantalising contact with smooth flesh just above the dress, where a little pulse was beating wildly. He stroked, she quivered, his body tightened in response.

Then came the rest of her, slender, flat-planed yet deliciously curvy inside the hugging dress. She was stretched out beneath him like an offering. But what exactly was on offer? Experienced lover or the beguiling innocent he'd walked away from on their wedding night and since suffered so many hot dreams about?

He slid his eyes back to her eyes, capturing a deep look of anxiety that pricked the hairs around his groin. The sultry heat of the afternoon shifted around them as he released a hissing sigh.

Time to find out. 'The answer is—no,' he stated very huskily then before the next stifled gasp could escape her he trapped it with his hungry mouth.

Nell felt herself go up in a plume of sharp static. The wait, the breathtaking silence, the scouring inspection of her body followed by his answer had shattered her tension and sent her spiralling out of control. Sensation latched on to every nerve-end, making each muscle she possessed stretch in long, sensual response then collapse into the driving power of his kiss.

He responded without hesitation, taking that kiss even deeper. It was as it had been in the water only far more demanding, a wild, escalation of pleasure that would not let her be still and had her fighting to free her trapped hands so she could touch him as he was touching her.

He let the hands go, sliding his own hand over her hair to the side of her neck then the smooth skin of the shoulder he had exposed for himself. His mouth followed, pressing small kisses to her skin that had her fingers clutching at his head. Smooth, dark silk hair filtered through her fingers. The kisses reached the soft, pulsing mound of her breast. She released a tight groan then pulled at his hair, caught his mouth and began kissing him back so desperately it was almost frightening.

'Want me?' It was so harshly spoken that Nell thought he was still angry; opening her eyes, she expected to see the cruelty of rejection about to hit her once again, only to find herself drowning in the smouldering, dark depths of desire.

'Yes,' she breathed.

His masculine growl scored her cheek as he plundered that soft, breathy answer, His hand returned to her shoulder, took a grip on the dress and pulled it down to her waist.

No bra—had he known that? The next masculine growl said yes, of course he had known it and long before he'd cupped her breast. He'd known from the moment she'd walked into the salon that she'd dared to come there wearing less than she should. Even her nervousness towards his mother had not been able to quieten the little devil at work inside her that wanted to torment him as she had been doing since he arrived in the cove.

His mouth took possession of one pouting nipple while his fingers took possession of the other. The wet and dry rasping of tongue and fingers sent her into a paroxysm of gasping jerks and quivers. He knew what he was doing. He knew this was torture.

'Xander.' She groaned out his name in an anxious plea for mercy and received it when his warm, damp mouth came back to hers.

After that she lost touch with everything but her senses and him. He was an expert at this and so incredibly ruthless about it she barely had time to absorb one new exciting experience before he was overriding it with something else. Her flesh sang where he caressed it, her restless fingers digging into satin-tight flesh that rippled in response to the sharp edges of her nails.

His shirt had gone. Nell had no idea that she had removed it. Her dress lay in a discarded heap on the floor. He was kissing her breasts again, her stomach, her navel, tongue-tip sliding sensual moisture across her acutely alive and sensitised flesh. When he suddenly rose to his feet, she let out a cry of pained protest because she saw rejection coming yet again. When she realised what he was doing, she moved on her side to watch him unashamedly as his fingers worked to free himself of the rest of his clothes.

Eyes black with promise, he watched her watch him. Every movement he made was hard and tense—packed with sexual motivation that curled her up with excitement. The trousers were stripped from his body and deep green eyes made a slow, shy sweep of him that couldn't help but linger on the bold thrust of his erection. Arrogant, she thought, and, on the tight little sensation of alarm mixed with excitement, she gave it the right to be.

'The way you look at a man is going to get you into trouble one day,' he ground roughly into the tension.

'I only do it with you.'

It was an admission that brought him back to her side, his superior framework rolling her onto her back so he could cover her. Then the real seduction of his bride began. It was hot and it was deadly serious, an intoxicating journey into a dark new world that explored all her senses and tuned them to a thick, throbbing, aching pitch. No tormenting of her breasts now but long, deep suckling, hands stroking her everywhere, the knowing movements of his body keeping her floating on a desperate high. When he finally eased the briefs down her legs then stroked his fingers along her thighs she began whimpering uncontrollably because she knew what was coming, her body clenching and unclenching in a mad mix of uncertainty and need.

He took her mouth in a deep, drugging kiss as if he knew what she was feeling and was trying to soothe her fears as he reached that warm, damp, untouched place. Her head suddenly filled with dark noises, a swirling, whipping, throbbing pulsation that had her fingers clutching at him. He was hot, damp, tense and trembling, his breathing all over the place.

'Nell.' He said her name, hoarse and husky, then made that first gentle intrusion inside.

She went wild in a second, it was that devastating. Had her gasping and crying out as shocking, hot pulses of pleasure rushed into her blood. He was touching her in ways that sent her mindless, smooth, slick, knowing fingers dragging feelings from her she would not have believed could be as powerful as this. And she could feel the heat of his own desire feeding from hers with the plundering depth of his kisses and the shuddering pleasure he was getting from this.

'Theos,' she heard him utter in a deep, rasping growl, then he stretched, the length of his sleek, muscled frame sliding damply against her. 'Nell...' He breathed her name like a caress, trying to reach wherever it was she had gone off to. 'I need to know if this is the first time for you.'

The first time, Nell repeated hazily, and lifted heavy eyelids to see the intensity burning in passion-glazed eyes and the savage control locked into his beautiful face.

'Of course it is,' she answered softly as if he should know that—and smiled.

His response was dynamic, the heated power of his kiss and the return of his caresses that drew her like liquid into thick, melting heat. She was lost and she knew it, blown away by sensation and the power he possessed to make her feel like this.

'Xander,' she whispered, feeling oddly as if he was slowly shattering her into tiny pieces.

He moved again, overwhelming in his maleness as he slotted himself between her thighs then made that first careful thrust with his hips. She felt his heat, his probing fullness. The shuddering strength with which he controlled the slow force of his entry was an experience in itself. Nell opened her eyes, found herself trapped once again by the spellbinding intensity carved onto his lean, dark features. He was big and bronzed and glossed with perspiration. The scent of his desire permeated the air. Sweat beaded his tautly held upper lip, his black eyelashes heavy over the bottomless black glaze of his eyes.

'You tell me if I hurt.' His voice was hoarse and husky.

She nodded, soft mouth parted, breathing reduced to small, thick gasps of quivering anticipation.

She felt the increased burn of his slow intrusion, the hunger, the reined-in control. Silken muscles flexed and he was trembling. She lifted her head to crush a kiss against his parted lips.

'Take it,' she whispered and the potent flare of masculine conquest lit his eyes when he made that final long, smooth stab that sent her arching against the bed in a moment of hot, stinging agony.

He caught the sound in his mouth as if it belonged to him, lips fusing like their bodies as she tensed and clawed at his hot, damp flesh that rippled with each helpless dig of her nails. His breathing was ragged, the tension holding him showing in the tremor of his fingers as they did their best to soothe the moment of discomfort away with gentle strokes of her face.

Yet, 'Mine,' he still breathed in rasping triumph, then the pain was dispersing and she was shifting restlessly beneath him. With a groan that lost him the final grip on control, he began to move again, plunging ever deeper while she made the wild leap into a mindless pleasure, clinging not clawing, riding the ever-increasing pace of his passion as it grew and grew until it exploded in a sense-shattering whirl of electrifying release. He followed her into that amazing place with convulsive rasps, which tore from his chest.

Too stunned by it all to do more than listen to the pounding of his heart as he lay heavily on her, Nell lay quietly beneath him while he laid languid kisses across her face.

'You surprised me,' he murmured.

'In what way?' She couldn't even find the energy to open her eyes as she asked the question.

His tongue teased her kiss-swollen bottom lip. 'You put me out of my misery when you could have damned me forever by letting me take you without knowing the truth.'

'Whether you are my first lover or not should make no difference.' She could not resist sliding her tongue across the tip of his.

'I am not built for innocence, *agape mou*.' He made a move with his hips so she could understand what he meant. He was still inside her, a thick, pulsing entity that filled her. 'I hurt you anyway, but not as much as I would have done without your generosity to keep me in check.'

'And your arrogance is showing again.'

'*Ne*,' he acknowledged lazily. 'But admit it—I did not disappoint.'

The remark was to remind her of her cutting little quip at the cove. Nell gazed up at him, watched him return the gaze with a dark-eyed, warm-lipped, wryly knowing smile. Beautiful, she thought helplessly, so indolently masculine and sure of himself. Her heart gave a hopeless little squeeze to let her know how much she still loved him despite every attempt she'd made to shut the feeling out.

Did he have any idea that the sex wasn't enough for her?

No, she was sure of it. He saw power in his undoubted physical prowess but wouldn't think to look beyond it for something deeper than that.

So what had she gained here?

Nothing, the hollow answer came back. If, that was, she didn't count intimacy wrapped around the kind of physical pleasure she never knew it was possible to experience.

For that alone she reached up to kiss him on the mouth. 'You didn't disappoint.' She was willing to grant him that much. 'Now all we have to do is wait to see if *I* disappoint...'

A frown grabbed his eyebrows, muscles flexing as he levered himself up on his forearms so he could narrow a questioning look into her face.

'You did not disappoint.' It was rough-toned declaration that vibrated across the walls of his cavernous chest and set her breasts tingling.

He was about to recapture her mouth when she added, 'I was talking about your other goal...'

'Goal?'

'To make me pregnant.' She spelt it out gently.

The comment acted like a cold douche on his lingering passions. He withdrew then rolled away from her. 'That was not my intention,' he denied.

'No?' Sitting up, Nell came gracefully to her feet then walked towards the bathroom on legs that felt too trembly and weak to carry her there, leaving that questioning little *no* hanging in the sultry air she left behind.

CHAPTER SEVEN

WATCHING her go, with her hair tumbling down her slender back helping to hide her nakedness from him, Xander wondered grimly how the hell she had walked him into that silken trap.

His body responded to tell him how. He hadn't used anything. He had not so much as glimpsed the distant idea of using anything to protect her from the risk of pregnancy—and not because of some fixed agenda he had been working towards, though he allowed Nell the right to believe that had been his ultimate motive. No, for the first time in his long sexual history he'd found himself too locked in the thrall of how she'd made him feel.

And if anyone from now on ever dared tell him that a condom did not stunt the pleasure of sexual intercourse then he would know they had never experienced what he had just experienced.

'Theos,' he breathed, turning it into a sigh as he threw himself flat against the bed then glanced down at his body, where the length of his shaft lay tight and proud against the flat of his abdomen, impatiently demanding more of the same.

It knew the difference. *He* knew the difference. He turned his head to glance at the closed bathroom door and wondered what Nell would say in response if he went in there and informed her that she had not been the only one enjoying a virgin experience in this bed.

Not one of his better ideas, he thought ruefully as that highly active part of his body gave another impatient tug. A confession like that would still not alter the fact that his intoxicating wife might be a virgin no more but her cynical view of him was still very much in tact.

And—hell, what could he say to make her believe that he'd harboured no deliberate intentions but had simply lost his head? The way his body was acting, it was not going to back him up. *It* wanted more—and more of what they'd just had. Prolific, rampantly free and potently unprotected sex shared with the beautiful, excitingly responsive woman who'd just left this bed.

Not just any woman—his woman.

His wife…

Sensation flipped a running ripple down his body. Turning his head on the pillow, he stared up at the ceiling where the lines of sunlight reflected on it filtered in through the slatted shutters then released a deep sigh of satisfaction at how good those two words sounded and felt.

His wife in fact and at last now in body. Why not enjoy sowing the seeds of that union? Why not tie the beautiful if cynical Helen to him so tightly she would never be free to attempt to leave him again?

See her walk away from their child-to-be with her Frenchman, he challenged grimly and felt hot, grinding jealousy stir in his chest. Who the hell was the guy that he believed he could poach his wife from him in the first place? *What* the hell did he have that made Nell want to go away with him so badly that she planned her escape a whole week before she crashed her car?

Then worse came, shifting him restlessly on the bed. Had the lily-livered swine chickened out at the last minute and Nell had been driving so fast because she'd been nursing a broken heart?

Did she love the guy?

Had she only let him make love to her here because she was thinking, what did it matter now?

It did not matter, he told himself. The Frenchman did not get her. He, Alexander Pascalis, did. Their marriage was consummated at last and whatever else came after this day, the one thing that would never change was that Nell now belonged to him right down to the last silken strand of hair on her beautiful head.

He settled back against the pillows, a look of grim calculation glinting behind his slowly drooping eyelids. The agenda was real. His cynical wife would have to get used to it because he was going to keep her barefooted and pregnant and too damn busy making love with him to pine for some fickle Frenchman who'd dared to break her heart.

That decision made, he relaxed his body, the sunlight glinting through the slats soothing in the soft, drowsy heat. In a second or two he would get up and join her in the shower he could hear running—consolidate his place with some very passionate seed-sowing and at the same time he would make Nell fall in love with him again. He could do it. She had loved him once. All it would take was some of his famous, single-minded ruthlessness to make her love him again…

Wrapped in a bathrobe, Nell stepped back into the bedroom to find the man of her dreams lying spread out on the bed and fast asleep. Her tummy muscles quivered at the picture he presented of bronze-muscled abandonment with his quietened sex still very much a daunting sight.

She'd half expected him to barge into the bathroom and demand she believe him that he had not deliberately set out to make her pregnant just now. Well, of course he hadn't. Any fool—even this fool called Helen Pascalis—could tell when a man was being ruled by his desires and not his intelligence.

Take note, darling Vanessa, she thought grimly. This man wanted me so badly that he couldn't stop himself from having me without the protection he stops to apply with you in bed. Now he sleeps on *my* bed with *my* kisses still moist on his skin and wearing the scents of *my* body on his warm golden flesh.

You're out, Vanessa, and I am most definitely in and with no intention of ever letting go. What I have right here, this time I keep.

It had taken her a whole year to recognise and understand that she had to fight for what she wanted instead of hiding away like some distant shadow waiting for Xander to remember that she lived.

Well, now she had him and she had no intention of letting

him go. A man who could tremble in her arms the way Xander had trembled was hooked and she knew it with every single fibre of her female being. And if she had to learn sensual wiles that were probably going to set her hair on end only to imagine them, then she was willing to use them to keep her man.

Before too long, Xander was going to find himself chained so tightly to her that he wasn't going to be able to take in a breath without her knowing about it. Instinctively her hand went to her cover her abdomen, inside which the seed of her lover was busily performing its potent magic—or if not yet it would be before too long.

A baby. Their baby. The next Pascalis heir. Eat your heart out, Vanessa, because this is one thing you will never have, she thought with grim satisfaction.

Ex-lover, she then corrected as she moved quietly towards the bed with a new deeply felt sensual pulse to her movements as she began to remove the bathrobe to begin her very first seduction of any man.

A sound coming from beyond the shutters diverted her attention; dropping the bathrobe to the floor, she crossed to the window to press a gap between two wooden slats and glanced down to see that Yannis was carrying out one of his daily duties and cleaning the pool.

Something else caught her attention. For a few short seconds she stood frowning, trying to decide what was different out there. Then her eyes alighted on Xander's helicopter where it stood anchored to its concrete deck—and alone.

A strangled gasp broke from her. She suddenly remembered the swirling, whipping noises as she'd lain in Xander's arms. Those sounds were not the sounds of the whirring, pulsating heat of their loving—they had been the sounds of his mother's helicopter leaving the island!

'Oh!' A blast of mortification at the way they'd left Gabriela kicking her heels downstairs while they made love up here had her whirling round to run to the bed.

'Xander...' It was necessary to put a knee on the mattress so she could reach his shoulder to give it an urgent shake.

'Wake up!' she insisted. 'Your mother has gone! You have to call her up and bring her back here. You—'

The snaking hook of a long, muscled arm toppled her onto him. 'Mmm,' he murmured sleepily. 'I was dreaming about you.'

'Will you listen?' she insisted, trying to fight him off and not to respond to the seeking warm brush of his mouth. 'I said your mother has gone!'

'I know.' The arm curved her closer. 'I heard her leave—didn't you?'

Nell flushed at what she'd believed the helicopter noise had been. 'You have to go and invite her back,' she said anxiously. 'She must be terribly offended to just go off like that.'

'You cannot offend my mother.' He was kissing her shoulder, the tip of his tongue gliding a sensual pathway towards her throat. 'Beneath the perfect gloss beats a heart of pure steel.'

Like the son; Nell frowned at the cool way he'd said that. 'Don't be cruel...'

'You taste of fresh water and soap.'

'I showered,' Nell mumbled distractedly.

'And removed my scent from your skin. Now I will have to put it back again.'

'But you need—'

'You,' he said. 'Again,' he added on a lusty growl as he leaned over to claim her mouth.

'Mmm,' Nell mumbled out a dizzy protest. 'Don't do that. Your mother. We have to—*What are you doing?*' she choked as his hand made a shockingly intimate dive between her legs.

'Making sure that you don't disappoint,' he returned smoothly, then laughed when her eyes widened in shock that he'd dared to actually admit it. 'A deal is a deal,' he said smoothly and flattened her to the bed.

Nell was caught in her own trap and she knew it.

When Xander had come back to the island to stake his claim on his bride, he did it by unleashing the full power of his sensual repertoire upon her that by far outstripped any ideas her naïve imagination she could have come up with.

He was amazing.

Any attempt to get him to talk about anything serious was thoroughly quashed by—sex. The kind of sex that could mercilessly slay her senses even when she was only thinking about it. He just had to look at her and she wanted him. He just had to say, 'Come here', in that rough-toned, desiring voice and she went like an eager lamb to the slaughter of her own common sense.

They played together, in the pool or in the ocean. He showed her how to reach the top of the rock flanking the little cove so they could dive into crystal-clear water beneath. He taught her how to fish from the selfsame rock then laughed himself breathless as she screamed in horror when she actually caught a fish.

And of course they made love—all the time, anywhere. Xander could not get enough of her and in truth Nell learned to use the newfound power over him with a feline ruthlessness that kept him forever and delightfully on his guard.

'I knew you would be dangerous once you discovered how to do this to me,' he complained late one afternoon after she'd spent the whole day taunting him with teases and half-promises and now rode him with slow and sinuous moves with her body that kept him pitched right on the edge, fighting not to give in because giving in before she did would fill her green eyes with so much triumph.

His skin was bathed in sweat and his hands were clamped to her supple hipbones. When she leant down to capture his mouth a whole new set of sensual muscles joined the torment. She caressed his taut cheekbones, the rasping clench of his jaw. She brushed the hard tips of her breasts against him and rolled her tongue around the kiss-softened contours of his lips before whispering, 'My lover,' then drew in every sensitised, beautifully tutored muscle to send him toppling over the edge.

As role reversals went, Nell knew she had cornered the market. She had him hanging on every flirtatious word and look and gesture like a besotted slave. On the occasions he grabbed back power just to remind her that he could do if he so desired to, she became the tormented one, the hopeless, helpless, besotted slave.

One week floated in perfect harmony into two then a third. Thea watched them and smiled a lot, and began crocheting an intricately patterned gossamer-fine christening shawl with a serene complacency that made Nell blush.

This was what she'd wanted, wasn't it?

Frowning as she bent to pick up a stray piece of driftwood off the shoreline, she sent experienced fingers gliding over its undulating ocean-smoothed contours the way her mother had taught her to do, while her mind drifted elsewhere.

She suspected she was pregnant. It was very early days yet to allow the suspicion to grow too large in her head, but her regular-as-clockwork period had let her down three days ago, and if Xander's virility was as potent as the rest of him then she knew, deep down, what it meant.

It changed everything. From believing she wanted to conceive his baby she now discovered that she didn't. Not yet, not like this. Not while they still hid from the real world on this tiny island where she felt more like a very indulged mistress than she did a wife.

A sigh broke from her, sending her chin tilting up so she could stare bleakly at the blue horizon. Xander could not remain hidden here for very much longer. As it was he needed to spend more and more time in his state-of-the-art study here dealing with business.

And Nell had pressing things of her own she needed to do—if she could only get to a telephone that did not have every call made on it carefully monitored.

Marcel. She was worried about him. She needed to know how he was and what he was doing. If he was cutting himself up with guilt and remorse or too angry with her to care that she was worrying about him.

When Xander did find it necessary to leave here, did he intend to take her with him this time or was she, in effect, still his prisoner whether it be behind the gates of Rosemere or here in this beautiful place?

He evaded the question each time she asked it. He evaded any discussion about life beyond here. Their honeymoon, he called it. A time to enjoy now, not what tomorrow had to bring.

But even a honeymoon as idyllic as this one had to come to an end some time.

She released another sigh. Xander watched it leave her as he stood in the window with the phone pressed to his ear. She was wearing a blue sarong today. Beneath the sarong would be a matching-coloured bikini, and her hair was up, looped into one of those casual knots she had a way of fashioning that always tempted him to tug it free.

His fingers twitched, so did other parts as he saw himself unwrapping the beautiful package that was his sensational, warm and willing wife.

Wife. *His wife.* As soon as he thought the words a blanket of seemingly unquenchable possessive desire bathed his flesh. He wanted to be out there with her, not standing here talking business on the telephone.

'I know I have to attend,' he snapped out, sudden impatience sharpening his tongue. 'I merely asked if there was any way it could be put back a week.'

No chance. He'd known it even before he suggested it. Wishful thinking was a useless occupation out there in the real world. And that was his biggest problem. Nell and this incredible harmony they had come to share did not belong in the real world. Nell, he'd come to realise, never did. Not in his world anyway. For the last year he'd kept her safely locked up inside a pair of iron gates, waiting, he'd told himself, for her to grow up before he attempted to redress the mess their marriage had become. In his arrogant self-confidence, he had not seen that she'd done the growing seething inside with resentment at the way he treated her. If she had not crashed her car, she would have been long gone with her Frenchman before he'd known anything.

And the way the guy had disappeared so completely turned

his blood cold when he thought of Nell disappearing with him like that.

'What of that other business?' he clipped into the telephone.

His frown deepened when an unsatisfactory reply came back.

'A man cannot drop from the face of the earth without leaving some trace, Luke,' he rasped out in frustration. 'I need you to find him. I need you to interrogate him. I need to know what his true intentions had been towards my wife!'

'And if it was a subtle form of kidnap?' he lanced back at whatever Luke Morell said. 'I will continue to think of her as in danger until I have answers... No, I will not leave her safety to the hands of bodyguards again. What use was Hugo Vance? Helen is my wife, my responsibility... Then let an empire crumble.'

Grimly he slammed down the phone, knowing he was being unfair, unwise—irrational. But how the hell else could he behave around a woman as unpredictable as Nell?

He'd spent three weeks in her constant company—had sunk himself into her more times than he cared to count! But did he know what made her tick? No more than he did a year ago when he'd wrongly believed he had her tagged and labelled—my beautiful, besotted wife.

She'd turned the tables on him that time. Then she'd done it yet again when she'd tried to leave him for her elusive Frenchman. OK, so this time he had managed to breach the damn citadel of her physical defences, but with Nell he could not afford to let the sex count for anything. He did not trust her, or that strange, glinting look he'd glimpsed in her eyes now and then. The little witch still had her own agenda, he was damn sure of it. She might love what he could make her feel, but did she love him...?

When you've had your fingers burned by complacency not once but twice, unless you are a complete fool you do not take chances on it happening again.

And what was she doing with that piece of driftwood? he questioned suddenly. The way she was caressing it was almost erotic. Was she imagining it was him—or someone else?

Jealousy. Uncertainty. He did not like feeling like this! With a grim clenching of every bone in him he spun away from the window, wondering what the hell he was going to do. He had to go to London. He did not want to take Nell with him. But was she going to accept that?

Not a chance in hell, he thought as he began gathering together papers that littered the top of his desk. Papers that were important to running an empire—yet all he wanted to do was hide away here with his wife!

A black scowl darkened his face as he strode into the hallway. Seeing Nell stashing the piece of driftwood by the open door, he pulled to a stop as he made one of those clean-cut, uncompromising decisions that usually made him feel better about himself.

'We need to talk,' he announced brusquely.

'We do?' Surprise lit her tone as she walked towards him, a sensational, wand-slender, Titian-haired woman wearing a halo of sunlight all around her. 'Well that makes a change,' she drawled teasingly.

He was wearing white, Nell noted. Xander liked to wear white, white, loose, fine muslin shirts that allowed the gorgeously tight, bronzed shape of his body show through, and white linen trousers that fastened with a tie cord low on his lean waist. One tug at the cord and she would reveal the real man, she thought temptingly, felt the hot secretion of desire sting her senses and wished she had more control over herself.

But she didn't and her mouth quirked into a rueful smile that acknowledged her weakness as she came to a halt in front of him and lifted her face for a kiss.

It didn't arrive. She focused her eyes on his hard, handsome face. He was cross, she realised. Her smile died.

'What was the smile for?' he demanded suspiciously.

'Well, it was for you but I've taken it back. What's the scowl for?' she countered.

He made an impatient flick with a long-fingered hand. 'I have to go to London today,' he told her abruptly.

London. Her eyes lit up. 'OK,' she said. 'So you don't have to sound so cross about it. I'll go and pack and we can—'

'No.' Xander used the refusal as if it were a landmine he was setting down in the small space between them. 'You will stay here.'

Nell's chin shot up again, green eyes making full contact with grimly uncompromising brown, then for the space of ten taut seconds she gave no response. Not with her steady gaze or her closed, perfectly formed mouth—or any other part of her, yet some inner body language had to be speaking to him because Xander tensed every muscle he had.

'It's business,' he clipped out as if that justified everything. 'I can be back here in two days. No need for both of us to uproot.'

'Do you want sex before you leave?'

It was not an invitation. In fact it was more like a cold slap in the face. The provocative witch, Xander thought heavily. 'Not if you are going to turn it into a punishment,' he returned drily, then grimaced because he was aware by the tingling of his flesh that he'd take the punishment if it was all that he was going to get.

'Goodbye, then,' she said and abruptly turned about.

She was going to walk away! Shock lanced through him. Didn't she care one way or another if he took her with him or not?

'Nell…' He rasped out her name not sure if it was said in anger or appeal. Then he took a step forward to catch her arm and the explosion erupted. She swung back, green eyes alive now and flashing with rage and biting contempt.

'What do you want from me, Xander?' she lashed out at him. 'Do you expect me to smile happily as I wave you off? Do you think I *like* knowing I'm a prisoner here, that I can only leave this island at your behest?'

'It's for your own safety.' He frowned darkly.

'For your peace of mind, you mean.'

'I have enemies! How do I know that your Frenchman isn't one of them until I locate him so that I can find out?'

'You mean—you're actually looking for him?' Her eyes went wide with shock.

His hooded. 'My people are.' He made yet another terse gesture with a hand. 'Your fate lies in what he has to say for himself.'

But his people hadn't found Marcel yet, Nell surmised from that and could not keep the relief from showing on her face.

Xander saw it. His own face hardened. 'You know where he is!'

She went to turn away again but his grip on her arm spun her back round. Defiance roared through her system. 'Don't manhandle me,' she protested angrily.

'Tell me where he is,' Xander hissed.

'Where's Vanessa?' she retaliated.

'This is not about Vanessa!'

'Well, I'm making it about her!' she flashed. 'Tit for tat, Xander,' she tossed back. 'You tell me all about your mistress and I'll tell you about my—'

'He was never your lover,' he derided before she'd even got the final word out.

But he wasn't denying that Vanessa was his! 'Not physically,' she conceded. 'But emotionally? How would you know if I love him? You wouldn't know about emotional love if it jumped up and bit you!'

The scorn in her voice had him tugging her towards him. Even as she landed hard up against his chest she was registering that something inside him had snapped. With ruthless intent he caught hold of the silken knot holding her hair up and used it to tug her head back then capture her angry mouth.

Titian silk crackled when it tumbled over his fingers as they strained against each other right there in the hall. Thin cotton beachwear was no barrier to hide what was happening to him but Nell was determined she was not going to give in to it. He was equally determined that she would.

A sound somewhere close intruded on the struggle. With an angry growl Xander scooped her up and swung her into his study, kicked the door shut behind them as he strode across the room to drop her on the soft leather sofa then followed her with his weight.

There the struggle continued. She plucked at his skin through his thin clothes with angry fingers, he forged a path with urgent fingers between her thighs.

'Stop it,' she gasped as his touch set her sobbing because she could feel herself responding even though she hated herself for it.

'Why?' he breathed tensely. 'This is not emotional enough? You think I go crazy like this for anyone? You think that you would feel hot and as willing as this for your Frenchman's touch?'

That he did not want an answer showed in the way he crushed her mouth open and plundered its sensitive interior. He was jealous of Marcel. He was doing this from the burning depths of a jealous rage. If she didn't stop him he was going to take her like this with none of the preliminaries then hate himself for it afterwards.

Closing her fingers in his hair, she pulled his head back to free her burning mouth. 'I think I'm pregnant,' she told him shakily, and watched as shock totally froze him, the colour draining out of his face.

In the pin-drop silence that followed neither of them took a single pounding breath, then Nell's mouth gave a vulnerable little quiver and he jackknifed away from her, landing on his feet by the sofa with his back towards her, muscles flexing all over him as he came to terms with what he had just been about to do.

Nothing like a good shock to turn the heat down, Nell thought bitterly and sat up, shaking fingers pulling her sarong back into place.

'Sorry to spoil your farewell,' she heard herself add with the slicing cut of embitterment.

His dark head jerked as if she'd hit him. In many ways Nell wished that she had. She had never felt so shocked and shaken. Without saying a word he just walked from the room.

Nell couldn't move. She thought he'd taught her everything

there was to know about making love but now she knew differently. A soulless slaking of lust that he dared to call emotion had not shown up in his repertoire before.

Nor had it prevented her from almost toppling into its cold, murky, thick depths. She started to shiver she was so cold suddenly, hating herself—despising him.

On the other side of the door Xander had frozen again, eyes closed, face locked into a taut mask of self-contempt. He did not want to believe that he had just done that. He did not want to remember the pained look on her face when she'd said what she said.

Pregnant. He flinched. What had he done here? How had he allowed three weeks of damn near perfection sink as low as this?

Marcel Dubois. The name arrived in his head like a black taunt.

No excuse, he dismissed. No damned excuse for doing what he had. The hand he used to scrape through his hair was trembling. Grimly he made for the stairs with a sudden dire need to wash the shame from his skin.

Nell was just trying to find the strength to stand up when the telephone on Xander's desk began to ring. She thought about ignoring it but something stronger than good sense pulled her like a magnet towards it and had her lifting the receiver off its rest.

When your life shatters, it really shatters, she thought blankly as a soft, slightly husky female voice murmured, 'Xander, darling? Is it all right for us to speak?'

The receiver clattered as it landed back on its rest. Pale as a ghost, Nell turned and walked to the door and out of the room then out of the house.

The piece of driftwood stood where she'd left it. Why she picked it up she hadn't a single clue but she hugged it to her front as she walked around the side of the house and took the path that would take her up the hill.

CHAPTER EIGHT

Two hours later, dressed for his trip to London in tailored black trousers and a crisp white business shirt, Xander gave up trying to locate Nell on foot and decided to take to the air instead. His mouth was tense, his lean face set and severe. He left an anxious-looking Thea standing by the pool, wringing her hands.

'Why did you have to fight with her?' she'd scolded him earlier. 'She's a good girl, Alexander. A trip to London to see her *papa* would not have put you out.'

The 'good girl' part was still cutting into him. The fact that Thea had overheard just enough of their fight to draw her own conclusions did not help his riddling feelings of guilt as the helicopter blades wound up, disturbing the hot morning as he took to the air.

Sat huddled on a rock hidden beneath the deep shade of a tree close to the spot from the one they usually dived from, Nell listened as the helicopter flew overhead.

He was going—leaving her here despite everything. Why she thought he might have a change of mind now he knew her suspicions about the baby she didn't know—but she had thought it.

Her eyes flooded with hot, helpless tears.

Vanessa. She shivered, feeling cold despite the fierce heat of the day. Perhaps his urgent business in London was really urgent Vanessa business. No wonder he'd become so angry when she wanted to go with him. What man wanted a wife along when he was looking forward to enjoying his long-standing mistress?

She hated him for treating her like this. She hated herself for falling so totally under his spell when she had known—

known that Vanessa was always there, hovering like the black plague in the background. A sudden husky, tear-thickened laugh broke from her aching throat. Face it, Nell, she told herself. You are the one he hides away like a mistress while Vanessa gets to play the very public wife!

Sweeping around the rocky headland, with deft use of the controls Xander swung the helicopter round to face the island then began to search the tiny cove.

She had to be here somewhere, he told himself grimly. Where the hell else could she go?

Dark glasses shading the brightness of the sun from his eyes, he checked the water first for sight of her but there was no sign of a Titian-haired mermaid swimming alone down there.

Teeth flashing white on a hiss of relief because if she was feeling anywhere near as bad as he was feeling she was in no fit state to swim alone, he switched his attention to the shore. He'd already checked the other side of the island, checked the paths through the trees without a single sighting of her. A viscous curse aimed at himself for introducing her to his boyhood collection of hiding places had led him on a wild-goose chase on foot. From up here it was like looking for a butterfly in a forest. If he did not spot her soon then he was going to panic. He could already feel it clawing at the inner tissues of tension racked across his chest.

What if she had decided to swim? What if she had been crazy enough to strike a direct line right out to sea? He swung the craft around, eyes scanning the glistening blue ocean for a sign of one wilful idiot with a desire to drown herself just to make him feel worse.

Don't be stupid, he then told himself. *Nell* isn't that stupid. And he uttered another curse as he swung the helicopter back to face the island then set it crabbing along the shoreline. She might hate him right now but not enough to risk killing herself—and their unborn child.

Their unborn child. A baby! He was still struggling to come to terms with the shock. His beautiful Helen was going to have his baby and he had never felt so wretched about anything in his entire life!

What had he done? *Why* had he done it? Jealousy was not an emotion he was used to. Women were jealously possessive of him, not the other way round!

Women, he repeated and let out a scornful huff of a laugh. *Woman* in the singular, he corrected. One tough, teasing, exquisite creature that fell apart in his arms on a regular basis yet still protected her bloody Frenchman!

What was he doing out there? Nell wondered as she watched him hover then move and hover again. Then enlightenment dawned. Why it took so long to sink in that he was looking for her she had no idea but, hugging the piece of driftwood to her, she lowered her head over it and squeezed her eyes tight shut and willed him to go away.

As if her wish was his command she heard him move further along the coast and for some totally indefensible reason the tears flooded again. She wouldn't cry—she wouldn't! she told herself forcefully as she listened to the dying whoosh of the rotor blades until only stillness filled the air.

Tomorrow she left here, she decided. She could do it and she knew exactly how. All it required was for her to feign illness and frighten poor Thea Sophia into calling in the air ambulance. She knew it could be done because she'd witnessed it happening when one of the maids had been taken ill suddenly during her first week here. The air ambulance had swooped in with a full complement of medical crew and efficiently carried the maid away.

Once she was away from this island she would disappear as thoroughly as Marcel had apparently done and to hell with Xander. She never wanted to lay eyes on him again.

Then, without warning, the helicopter was back and suddenly so close that her chin scraped the driftwood as her head shot up. By then Xander had inched the machine in so close to the edge of the ledge that for a horrible moment she truly believed he was going to crash!

Leaping to her feet, she ran to the edge on some crazy idea that she could make him stop!

For a hellish kind of moment Xander thought she was going to take to the water. Icy dread bathed his flesh as he looked down at the sea where the ebbing tide had uncovered the razor jutting peaks of some lethal rocks.

'Get back, you fool!' he heard himself bellow at the top of his ragged voice, almost lost control of the helicopter and, by the time he'd wrestled with it and looked back at her, she was already teetering on the edge and caught up in a whirlwind of dry, stinging dust and flying debris, her slender frame cowering as she stared at him in abject horror.

Teeth lashed together, he pushed in closer, herding her backwards step by unsteady step until she was safely back from the edge. Then he stayed there, hovering so dangerously close that if he didn't harness nerves of steel he had a feeling it would be him tumbling to his death.

Shaken, severely shaken when she realised what Xander was doing, Nell began to back away, so terrified for him she took the stinging whip of dust full in the face while she screamed at him to move back!

The whole mad, nerve-slaughtering incident could only have used a few seconds but by the time she saw him begin his retreat she was close to fainting with relief.

Xander kept his jaw locked tight as he swung the machine away. If he could he would land on the damn beach so he could run up there and strangle life out of her for being so stupid, but there were too many overhanging branches covering the narrow crescent of sand to make it a safe place to land.

Biting out a thick curse, he flew back round the island to land by the house. Having settled the machine down, he then just sat there, bathed in sweat and shaking too badly to move. What if she'd jumped? What if the rotor blades' fierce downdraft had toppled her over the edge?

He climbed out of the cockpit. His legs felt hollow as he walked. The sun was hot but his skin wore the chill of stark, mind-blowing fear.

What next? What now…?

He knew what now, he told himself grimly as he set his feet walking in the direction of the pathway that would take him up the hill.

Nell saw the helicopter was safely back on its pad as soon as she crested the peak of the hill and her footsteps stilled. She'd thought Xander had gone. She'd *hoped* he had gone. Now she could see that he hadn't, her instincts were telling her to flee back into the woods and find a new place to hide from him.

Then the man himself appeared, rounding a bend in the path below, sunlight filtering through the trees to dapple his long frame dressed in smooth black trousers and a crisp white business shirt with a slender dark tie knotted at his brown throat. When he saw her he pulled to a stop.

He looked every inch the lean, dark Greek tycoon, Nell thought sinkingly. Hewn from rock, and twice as hard.

Lowering her eyes, she hugged the piece of driftwood even tighter to her chest then took some short, shallow breaths to help her feet to move.

He waited, watching her from behind the shade of his silver-framed sunglasses, the rest of his face caught by a stillness that worried her more than if he'd come charging like a bull up the hill. She'd always known that Xander could be tough, cold, ruthless. She'd always been aware of that streak of danger lurking inside him that was sensible to be wary of. But even on those few occasions when she'd sensed the danger had been threatening to spill over she'd never really expected him to give in to it. Now he had—twice in as many hours. First back at the villa then up there on the rock ledge when he'd driven the helicopter right at her without a care for his own safety.

Now she did not know what to expect from him—didn't want to know. If she possessed the luxury of choice she would not even want to be even this close to him again.

As it was her feet kept her moving down the path until she drew to a halt about six feet away from him. Tension sparked in the sun-dappled silence, and kept her eyes focused on a point to the right of his wide, white-shirted chest.

Xander felt the muscle around his heart tighten when he saw the chalky pallor pasting her cheeks. He knew he'd frightened her with the helicopter manoeuvre. Hell, he'd frightened himself! *She'd* frightened him. Now all he wanted to do was gather her into his arms and just hold her close, but what had come before the fright on the rocky ledge had lost him the right to do that.

'I thought you'd gone.' She spoke first, her voice distant and cool.

'No.' He, on the other hand, sounded raw and husky. 'Are you OK?'

She gave no reply as if the answer spoke for itself. She was not OK. Looking into those carefully lowered, beautiful eyes set in that beautiful face, he thought it was as if a light had gone out. He'd switched it off. Now he didn't know what to do or say that would switch it on again.

Dragging off his sunglasses, he pushed them into his trouser pocket then gripped them in a strangling clinch. 'What's with the piece of driftwood?' he asked out of a need to say something, however inane.

The bewildered way she glanced down at the piece of sun-bleached wood hugged close to her chest, he had a suspicion that she'd forgotten it was there.

'N-nothing,' she mumbled. 'I—like it.'

She liked it...

This was crazy! They'd almost killed each other not ten minutes ago; now here they were, standing halfway up a hill discussing bloody driftwood when they should be—

'Shall we go down?' he suggested on a thick, driven rasp.

She nodded, lowered her eyes all the way to the ground and pushed her feet into movement again. When she drew level with him he fell into step beside her and the tension inside him pounded in his chest as they walked side by side without uttering another damn word.

When they reached the house, Thea was standing anxiously in the doorway.

'Oh, there you are!' She hurried forward to close Nell's pale face between gnarled fingers in a gesture of relief. 'Alexander was so worried when he could not find you. The foolish boy went crazy, upsetting everyone by turning the whole house upside down and searching the wood before he jumped in his helicopter to look for you from the air.'

The *foolish boy* stood by in grim silence while Nell quietly soothed the old lady's anxious nerves. 'I was walking on the other side of the island,' she said gently.

'This explains why you did not hear us calling to you.' Thea nodded. 'Now you must hurry and change out of those beach clothes or he will grow truly impatient and go without you.'

Nell started frowning. 'Go where?' she asked.

'With Alexander to London, of course!' Thea exclaimed in beaming triumph. She turned to her great-nephew. 'Did you not tell her that you have changed your mind?' Then before he could answer she was hustling Nell inside. 'Come—come. Your case has been packed for you. All you need to do is choose something to wear to travel in, then we...'

Nell was glancing back over her shoulder, a puzzled frown on her face. Xander was saying nothing—nothing, and his grim, dark stance did not encourage questions.

What was going on? Why had he changed his mind? 'Xander—'

'Do as Thea says,' he cut in. 'We must leave in ten minutes if we are to make our air slot out of Athens.'

With that he spun and strode away.

Bewildered and confused, Nell allowed herself to be hurried upstairs. Xander had to have decided to take her with him before he started looking for her but—why?

'You must not get so upset when he lets off the anger, *pethi mou*,' the old lady murmured beside her. 'He loves you. That makes him jealous and possessive. All Pascalis men are the same. He worries that you might meet some other fine young man in London and leave him—as if you would be so cruel...'

Nell felt a blush stain her cheeks at Thea's faith in Nell's loyalty to her great-nephew, because she knew that she could be so cruel—*would* be so cruel if she was given the opportunity.

This marriage was over as far as she was concerned.

The flight to Athens airport was quick and smooth and trouble-free. As they flew across the island before heading towards the mainland, Nell didn't even bother to glance down.

She'd come to love that little island but she would not be coming back to it. And her only regret at leaving it behind was having to leave a tearful Thea behind too.

'You will come and see me soon,' the old lady made her promise. Nell didn't have the heart to say no, never again.

Landing in Athens was like being dropped from heaven into hell. The moment they began the transfer from helicopter to waiting plane, people stopped to stand and stare. Xander didn't seem to notice. Nell had a feeling he didn't see anything beyond his next target, which in this case was his private plane waiting on the tarmac.

With only a few minutes to spare to hit their slot, they boarded the plane and were taxiing towards the runway only moments after they'd strapped themselves into their seats.

And the whole shift from island to plane had been achieved in an empty hollow of perfect silence. It was awful. Neither spoke, neither attempted to, neither looked at the other. Body language did it all for them. Dressed in a razor-sharp business suit, he was grim, tight-lipped and supremely contained within himself.

Nell, on the other hand, had nothing she wanted to say. She was wearing the same clothes she'd travelled to Greece in—mainly because they were hanging in the closet and she hadn't cared what she wore so long as she got back down the stairs within the allotted time. The only difference being that her hair had been left loose because she didn't dare waste time in braiding it in case he left the island without her. As she'd walked out into the sunshine where Xander was waiting for her, he'd taken one look at her from behind those miserable sunglasses, his mouth had compressed then he'd just turned and stridden away.

She'd suffered his help into the helicopter without flinching and kept her gaze fixed directly ahead as he settled himself in his seat. Tension had fizzed all around them throughout the short hop to Athens Airport—making it almost impossible to breathe.

Now they sat surrounded by the kind of luxury travel most people only read about, yet they could have been two strangers on a packed package flight, the way they sat across the aisle from each other, ignoring the other's presence. As soon as the plane levelled out Xander was climbing to his feet. The sunglasses had gone but it made no difference; his long, glossy eyelashes had taken their place and Nell refused to look up at him anyway.

He disappeared into his custom-built office area towards the back of the plane and a smiling Greek stewardess brought Nell refreshment—at Xander's instruction, she presumed, because no one had asked her if she wanted anything.

Still, the freshly brewed tea was like manna from heaven after her having drunk nothing for hours. And she even managed to nibble at the selection of freshly made sandwiches before she gave up and pushed the tray away. After that she spent some time flipping through a couple of magazines without focusing on a single page. Then, in the end, because she felt so utterly dragged down and exhausted by all the emotional stresses, she rested her head back against the seat and went to sleep.

When she eventually opened her eyes again she found Xander standing over her. Her nerve-ends leapt on edge, her defences shooting back into place so violently that what she'd gained by managing to fall asleep was lost in that instant.

A nerve ticked in his jaw as she glanced warily up at him. He quickly flicked his eyes away. 'We will be landing at Heathrow in twenty minutes,' he informed her then strode away, his body language still speaking loud and clear.

The walk through Heathrow was like being placed beneath a microscope. As had happened in Athens, people stopped in their droves and stared. Nell wanted to curl into a tight chrysalis and just—disappear. With a trio of tough-faced bodyguards hustling around them, they must look like one of those celebrity couples you saw splashed across the tabloids. She hated it and kept her eyes lowered and was actually grateful for the protective arm Xander placed around her as he paced beside her like a sleek, prowling cat that wanted to leap off and savage a couple of those staring faces—keeping up appearances, she thought again with a tiny grimace. And wondered curiously why she hadn't been treated to this kind of walk down the concourse when they'd left London for Greece. But didn't ask; neither the man nor the moment nor the throat-clutching pump of her heartbeat encouraged speech.

Rico was waiting outside with the Bentley, its rear door held open wide. She was hustled inside the car's luxury interior, Xander followed, the door shut, silence clattered around them with the same ear-twisting quality of a full string orchestra tuning their instruments.

They sped away with all the smooth efficiency Xander clearly took for granted. Nell would have smiled if she'd had the will to but she didn't. She had never felt as cold and unhappy or as isolated—and that was saying something, she mused as she stared out of the car window.

'Do you actually like living like this?' The words were out before she could stop them.

'I beg your pardon?' That she had surprised him with real speech showed in the huskiness of his voice.

'Like you're a beast living in a zoo,' she enlightened and watched him stiffen. 'Or maybe you're the star in the quintessential TV reality show,' she went on, wishing she'd kept quiet, but unable to stop herself from going on. 'Everything you do, wherever you are in the world, is watched and discussed and pored over. The Press love you. Those people back there love you. Paths appear in thick crowds so you can pass through unhindered while they stand and goggle and gasp.'

She dared to flick a look at him then wished she hadn't. He was sitting like a block of rock, no reaction whatsoever. It infuriated her; she didn't know why but it did.

'Is there a weekly vote on who gets kicked out of your life next?' she prodded recklessly. 'Do big companies fall to a million or two phone calls? Mistresses get dumped—bodyguards that don't fit the tough-guy bill?'

'Shut up, Nell,' he advised very quietly.

She wished she could but she was on a roll here. 'If I don't please the masses, do I get to go too? Vote out the nagging little wife so our wonderful hero does not have to listen to her any more!'

She saw his hands curl into two fists on his lap. 'You are going nowhere, so don't build your hopes up.'

'Because I might be pregnant?' she flashed at him with acid bite. 'Well, that event should boost the ratings. Do we produce your son and heir in front of a blaze of cameras and maybe have your mistress watching from the sidelines just to add a bit of spice?'

The snakelike twist of his body came without warning. For such a big man he struck with stunning, lithe grace. Before she even knew what was happening he had her trapped in the corner of the seat with a hand at her nape and the other clamped across her reckless mouth.

'Now listen...' he hissed out in thin warning.

Nell stared at him over the top of his clamping hand—really stared, and for the first time took in his pallor, the tension cutting deep grooves around his wide, sensual mouth. But it was his eyes that held her, eyes like black crystal that pierced her so sharply they hurt.

'I give you the right to mock me and my lifestyle,' he bit out tautly. 'I will even admit that I probably deserve to feel the acid whip of your tongue. But you will not mock yourself in the same manner and you will *not* degrade our unborn child!'

Is that what she'd done? Oh, yes, that was what she had done, Nell acknowledged. Her lips trembled beneath his hand.

'And don't cry,' he added on a driven mutter. 'I have enough torment to contend with without you adding your tears!'

Her breasts heaved on a tightly suppressed and tremulous shudder. Some of that torment he'd admitted to flashed across his eyes. He bit out a couple of thick foreign curses then, with the same unpredicted lithe movement, let go of her and snaked back into his own seat.

'You have no idea what you do to me,' he said then in rough-toned fury while Nell just sat there and trembled. 'You have no idea of your own damn power to draw breathless gasps from the masses!'

Shocked by that, she blinked at him in bewilderment. Turning his dark head, he caught the surprised blink and his lean face hardened into cynicism.

'You have the wild, waving hair of a fantasy mermaid, the face of an angel and the body of a natural sensualist!' he ripped out as if in contempt. 'Your sensational legs are so slender and long there isn't a man alive that would not have hot dreams about them wrapped around him. Other women look at you and *wish* they possessed a small fraction of what you've got! *I* wish I'd never set eyes on you, then I would not be sitting here feeling hard and hot and bloody frustratingly impotent to do anything about it!'

'Trust you to drag it all down to your lower-body level,' Nell responded, too shaken by what he'd thrown at her to care that her voice quivered with the onset of fresh tears. '*I* wish you'd never set eyes on me too, then I would not have spent the last year being shipped from one luxury prison to another by a money-motivated brute with sex on the brain!'

'So what would you rather have been doing?' he questioned curiously.

'Getting on with my life!'

'Life with the Frenchman perhaps?'

Turning a tight-lipped profile to him, she refused to answer. Let him think what he liked about Marcel, she thought mutinously—especially if it annoyed the hell out of him!

'Tell me, Nell, because I'm genuinely curious. Did the elusive pimpernel have the fifty million to bail your father out?'

'Marcel is not motivated by money,' she stated haughtily.

'Ah, so he's dirt poor with a sensitive heart but no balls,' he said crudely.

Nell flashed him a disgusted look. 'You know nothing about him so don't pretend that you do.'

'Are you so sure about that?'

'Yes!' she insisted. 'Or you would have had him beaten up by your mob and be throwing it at me by now.'

'Clever girl,' he drawled.

'Shut up.' She hated him.

'Are you going to tell me where he is?' he persisted.

'You must be joking,' she scoffed.

'No,' he denied. 'In fact I have never been more serious. Where is he, Nell?' he repeated levelly. 'And before you answer me with some whipping comment I think I should warn you that your freedom will continue to be restricted until you do tell me...'

Nell sizzled on a seething breath of air. 'I wish I'd never married you.'

'As if your choices were crowding at your father's begging door,' he mocked. 'As far as I am aware, it was either me or some short, ugly guy in his forties with fat lips and three pairs of hands.'

Stung, she flicked him a sharp glance. 'What's that supposed to mean?'

'Nothing—forget I said it.' Frowning, he leant forward to press a button, which brought a miniature drinks bar shooting out of the car's central bulkhead.

Feeling a bit as though she was about to be slaughtered where she sat, Nell watched him select a bottle of whisky then pour himself a measure into a squat crystal glass. He relaxed back into the seat, downing some of the whisky as he went, his lean face turned to stone again with just the merest hint of self-contempt.

Nell's upper lip trembled as she parted it from her stiff lower lip. 'Xander, y-you—'

'Don't ask,' he clipped out.

But it was too late. He had not pulled that nasty remark out of a bag at random just to get at her. There had been hard meaning behind every deriding word.

'I n-need to know what you meant.'

'You married me, therefore it meant nothing.' He stared grimly into his glass.

'Tell me!' she cried.

A burning blast of annoyance racked his face. 'Your father had overstretched his resources. He was sinking very fast. He needed bailing out but there are not many people out there with fifty million pounds sterling to spare on a very bad risk. I was one such person willing to take the risk—for a price.'

Julian Garrett's daughter and his risky investment protected as much as it could be with the production of a son and heir from the union who would claim the daughter's inheritance!

'You already know all of this, so why drag it all out again?' Xander flicked harshly into the strumming tension holding Nell pale and still.

Because he was still missing out one vital detail—the man with the fat lips. The weekend before Xander came to stay at her father's house, Clive Benson had come to stay—short, overweight, constantly smiling. At first she'd suffered his over-friendly attitude towards her out of good manners and because she thought he was just doing it in a fatherly way—until he'd become just a bit too friendly, and dared to touch her thigh. She'd taken refuge by spending as much time as she could outside with the dogs, aware that her father had some heavy business going with the man—aware that she could not afford to offend.

'You're trying to imply that my father put me up for auction,' she whispered.

'You will please make note that I am trying hard *not* to say those ugly words, *agape mou*,' he returned.

But they were there—they were there!

'My father wouldn't do such a h-horrible thing to me.'

Silence. All Xander did was toss the rest of his whisky to the back of his throat. Nell felt the churning surge of nausea in her stomach.

'I w-wouldn't have Clive Benson touch me w-with a barge-pole.'

'I am so relieved that I did not encourage such feelings of objection,' Xander drawled. 'But take a moment to consider what you would have done if I had not offered a rescue package. Without me or—someone else to bail him out, your father's company, his employees and countless other subsidiaries would have gone under and sunk without a trace. He would have been in debt to his eye-teeth. His bullish pride would have been shattered. His home would have gone and his beautiful daughter would have found herself tossed out on the street. Suddenly wealthy men like Clive Benson don't look so bad, hmm?'

'Stop the car,' Nell breathed thickly.

He looked utterly incredulous. 'We are travelling on the motorway!' he laughed, then he saw her milky pallor and his voice roughened. 'For goodness' sake, Nell, it's too late for you to run away from—'

'Stop the car!' she all but shrieked at him just before her hand jerked up to cover her mouth.

To give him his due, when he realised what was about to happen he moved like lightning, wrenching forward to snatch up the internal telephone and snapping out the order to Rico. Nell all but fell out of the car, staggering on wobbly legs across the hard shoulder of the motorway before she was thoroughly and violently sick onto the grass verge.

The arms that came to take her weight and keep her hair back at the same time were a godsend. She didn't even care that he had to stand there watching her bring up the full contents of her heaving stomach. She'd never felt so wretched— or so distressed. Everything he'd said and *not* said was pulsing and throbbing inside her.

When it was over she folded at the knees. In grim silence

Xander picked her up and resettled her on the back seat of the Bentley with her feet still out on the tarmac. He began snapping out orders while Nell desperately wanted to gulp in some deep lungfuls of fresh air but didn't dare do it in case she set the nausea off again. She was shaking like crazy. Even when Xander squatted down in front of her and gently urged her to sip the cool water that had appeared from nowhere, she still couldn't stop shaking like a leaf.

'My bag,' she managed to push out thickly.

He didn't question the request, just reached inside and found her bag where she'd placed it on the car floor and silently laid it on her lap. Her trembling fingers fumbled with the catch as she tried to open it. She could *feel* Xander wanting to take it and do the clasp for her but he didn't give in to the urge. Maybe he knew that even a small thing like that was going to tip this awful situation right over the edge.

The clasp sprang open; fingers scrambling inside, she found the little plastic envelope of damp freshen-ups she always carried, and managed to peel one away from the rest. Her hair was hanging all over her face and she was glad to have it hide the ravages she knew were there. I will never look at him again, she vowed sickly as she used the damp tissue to wipe her face, then she took the cool glass of water from him and began sipping sparingly while he continued to squat there with his hands clenched in fists between his spread thighs.

'OK?' he questioned her huskily after a few more minutes.

She nodded, offering the glass back to him, but didn't attempt to lift her head. Other things began to impinge on her consciousness, like the sound of other cars roaring past them on the motorway and the other car pulled up bumper to bumper with theirs. The three tough bodyguards had positioned themselves at a discreet but protective distance around the car.

She couldn't even be spared the dignity of privacy while she was sick.

'Nell, I'm sorry. I didn't say all of that to—' One of his hands was lifting towards her.

'Don't touch me.' She withdrew from him like a tortoise retracting into its shell.

Swivelling her legs into the car, she just sat motionless while he remained squatting there, the pull on the air so taut it felt as if it could wrench her in two.

He stayed like that for a few more seconds then rose to his full height. The car door closed, Nell used the few seconds it took him to stride around the car to comb her hair away from her face with trembling fingers. He arrived in the seat beside her, Nell turned her face to the side-window. The bodyguards dispersed. Car engines fired and the journey towards London continued in perfect—perfect—silence.

She must have dozed off, though she didn't remember doing it, but the next thing she knew the car had pulled to a stop outside a row of London townhouses sporting polished brass plates on the walls by the doors.

'Where are we?' she questioned. But Xander was already climbing out of the car. By the time he opened her door for her then stood there in grim silence waiting for her to get out, Nell had worked out exactly where they were.

'I don't need a doctor,' she protested.

The hand that took a grip on her arm said everything as he all but lifted her with it out of the car. He walked her up the steps and in through a doorway, where she glimpsed the word 'Gynaecologist' on one of the plaques with a sinking heart.

'It's too soon to consult anyone about…'

Half an hour later, with her grim-faced companion's hand like an electric charge to the hollow of her back, she was walking out again feeling washed-out and wasted and close to tears.

It was confirmed. She was pregnant. About three weeks along, at a considered guess. Potent didn't even cover it. He'd managed to achieve his goal at first try, knowing him, she thought bitterly.

'Mission accomplished,' she said in a voice that dripped ice, then stepped away from that proprietary hand and walked alone to the waiting car.

CHAPTER NINE

XANDER sat beside her as the car swept them onwards and wished to hell that he knew what to do to break this bloody grip guilt had on his conscience. In one short day he had managed to obliterate three weeks of total heaven.

He didn't want to feel like this!

He didn't want to look at her only to see that pained expression she'd worn on her pale face when the doctor had confirmed her pregnancy. He'd seen the same expression once already today when she'd been forced to tell him her suspicions about their baby because she knew it was the only way she would have stopped him taking her like a rutting beast!

In a zoo.

Theos. She had never spoken a truer word to him. How do you approach a woman who saw you like that?

How did you look her in the face when you'd just bludgeoned her with the ugly truth about her father?

You don't, came the tough but true answer. You back right off if you have a drop left of civilised blood. You put your stupid, juvenile burn of jealousy over the bloody Frenchman back under wraps, then take up the happy task of slowly and painfully trying to rebuild trust.

He turned his face to the side-window. Everything inside him felt as if it was carved in stone. One minute more of this God-awful silence and he was going to explode!

Relief arrived when he saw the front of his super-modern smoked-glass office building loom up beside the car. Rico got out and opened his door for him. Xander climbed out then moved round the car with the *civilised* intention of assisting Nell to alight, but she did that on her own.

He said nothing, took her arm, she flinched then settled. In a strained way he thanked her for that, and kept his own flinching contained inside. As they walked together through the smoked-glass doors into the vaulted foyer he saw the zoo analogy come up and hit him in the face like a bloody great tank.

Glass everywhere, cold tungsten steel. People—*employees*, for God's sake—stopping what they should be doing to turn and stare. He felt Nell quiver, his fingers twitched on her slender arm. Behind his grim lips his teeth were biting together so tightly they hurt as he walked her across the foyer and into the executive lift. The doors closed. They were transported upwards with ultimate speed. She stared at the floor, he stared at the wall half an inch to the side of her head.

And the hell of it was that he was willing her to look at him, *willing* her to make that slow, sensual journey up from his polished shoes to his face.

It didn't happen. He'd never felt so bloody bereft.

The doors swished open. Nell had to steel herself to accept the return of his hand on her arm. Inherent Greek manners demanded that he hold her like this but she wished he were walking ten feet away.

She had never been inside this building before, definitely never been up here in his spacious and plush executive domain. More glass and steel met her gaze, interspersed now with panels of rich walnut and yet more curious faces that kept her eyes glued to her shoes.

The murmured greetings delivered with respect echoed the length of the long walk down the corridor. Xander said nothing. He was like a mechanical machine delivering a package.

Then his hand moved from her arm to the centre of her back as he leant forward to open a pair of huge walnut doors. She felt his fingers slide into the weight of her hair and for a moment—a brief, sense-grabbing moment—his fingertips curled then straightened on a sharply compulsive sensual stroke.

Her breathing froze. She looked up at him. She hadn't wanted to do it but now it was too late and he was looking down. Everything stopped—*everything*! The door, only half pushed out of its housing, the sea of faces they'd left in their wake. He stood at least six inches taller than her and she wished—wished—*wished* she hated that handsome dark face!

Her eyes began to blur with stupid tears, her mouth started to quiver.

'Nell, don't,' he murmured thickly then turned like a whip on the sea of faces. 'Have you nothing better to do than to watch me make love to my wife?'

Shocked by the sudden outburst, Nell drew in a sharp breath. Muffled sounds erupted behind them. Xander bit out a curse then pushed the door wide and propelled her inside.

She found herself standing in a huge walnut-panelled office with a wall of glass, a steel-legged desk and a vast expanse of polished floor. The door shut with a controlled thud. As soon as it happened Nell spun around.

'What made you shout that out?' she demanded shrilly.

'Even zoo animals get sick of being stared at,' he rasped.

He had a grip on her hand now and was trailing her behind him across the room towards another set of double doors while, in a near-dizzy state of too many shocks in a single day, Nell found herself struggling with pangs of remorse.

'Look, I'm sorry I said that,' she said stiffly.

'It was only the truth. I do live in a zoo.'

A telephone started ringing somewhere. In a state of complete disorientation, Nell found herself being trailed in a different direction, towards the desk, where whole rows of paperwork stood lined up in thick, neat stacks. In amongst the stacks was the ringing telephone. Xander hooked it up with his free hand and began a clipped conversation in Greek.

She tried to slip her hand free but he refused to let go of it. The moment he replaced the receiver it started ringing again. Keeping her firmly anchored to him, Xander embarked on a series of conversations as one call led to another then another.

As one call stopped and before another started, Nell drew in a deep breath. 'Look, you're busy. And I need...' to lie down, she had been going to say but changed her mind because lying down meant a bed, and she didn't want to think about beds. 'If you'll let me use the limo, I'll go down to Rose—'

'You stay with me.' It was not up for argument. 'We are not—'

The phone shrilled out its demand for his attention. On a growl of annoyance Xander snatched it up. 'Hold the calls until I say otherwise!' he instructed, the bark of his voice rattling the windows.

Nell winced. 'I *hate* bullies.'

'Tough.' She was being trailed across the floor again. 'The vote's still out on your fate, so you stay.'

It took Nell a few seconds to get his meaning. 'Will you stop throwing my words back in my face?'

By then he'd taken them through that other pair of doors and her attention was seized, because this was no office but some kind of beautiful sitting room decorated and furnished to Xander's impeccable high standards and luxurious good taste.

'What is this place?' she asked curiously.

'My apartment.'

'You mean *this* is your City place?' She sounded so surprised that he sent her a wry look.

'What did you expect—some purple and red velvet-lined pad in atmospheric Soho specifically designed for bedding my women?'

The bedding-of-his-women bit brought the lovely Vanessa right into full focus. Instantly her face turned to paste.

He saw it and bit out a sigh. 'When I'm in town I work, I crash out here, I work,' he enunciated abruptly. 'I also keep a place in the country but have never got to sleep there yet.'

His sarcasm was really on a roll, Nell noted heavily, and was suddenly fighting yet another battle with tears… The next thing she knew she was being engulfed by a pair of arms, her face pressed to his chest.

'Idiot…'

The husky tone of his voice rumbled right through her. She wasn't sure who was the idiot, her or him, but she did know she wanted to be right where she was right now, and that had to make her a complete idiot.

The small haven of comfort didn't last long though. 'Come on,' he said gruffly, and turned her beneath the crook of his arm to guide her through yet another set of doors into a— bedroom with a huge, smooth coffee and cream covered bed on which he urged her to sit down on the edge.

'Now listen,' he said, coming to squat down in front of her. 'It's been a hell of a day and you're exhausted. The wise doctor advised rest so you will obey him and rest—alone *agape mou*,' he added severely at the protest he'd already predicted was about to shoot from her lips. 'I have work to do, consisting of a mountain of paperwork to plough through before I chair a meeting in...' glancing at his watch '...less than an hour.' Grimacing, he sprang lithely to his feet. 'There is a bathroom through that door,' he indicated. 'And a kitchen adjoining the other room if you feel the need for sustenance...'

He was already over at the window and drawing the curtains, so disgustingly invigorated by the prospect of work, while all Nell wanted to do was crawl into this bed and sleep.

'If you need me for anything,' he said as he walked back to her, 'there is a telephone in every room. All you have to do is hit the one button and you will reach me. OK?'

Locating the telephone on the bedside cabinet, Nell looked at it wistfully. 'Can I ring out on it?'

'No, you cannot!' He was suddenly in front of her and taking her shoulders to pull her upright. 'Now, listen, you aggravating bundle of controversy. I am in no mood to fight with you any more today, but if you attempt to contact your ex-lover I'll fight hard and dirty—got that?' He gave her a gentle shake.

'Yes,' she said.

He let go of her with an impatient hiss. 'Go to bed, get some rest and stop wishing for miracles.'

With that he strode out of the room with his dark head held high and his wide shoulders straight, leaving Nell wilting wearily back onto the bed.

Less than ten minutes later, stripped to her underwear, she crawled between the cool Egyptian cotton sheets. Feeling utterly bulldozed, she simply closed her eyes and dropped into sleep.

Pregnant, was her last memorable thought. I really am pregnant…

Pregnant, Xander was thinking as he stood in the doorway, following the streaming cascade of Titian hair spread out on the pillow until his gaze settled on her pale, pinched, sleeping face.

Was he pleased?

Hell, he didn't know. He wanted to be pleased. He wanted to shout it from the rooftops. But when he looked upon the face of this—impossible woman, he had a sinking suspicion that the cost he was going to pay for the pleasure of impregnating her was going to be much too high.

Smothering a sigh, he eased himself away from the doorframe and stepped back into the sitting room, pulling the door quietly shut.

Time to stop playing the lovelorn idiot, he told himself, and time to play the hard-hitting, go-getting business tycoon.

A role he was much more familiar with. A role he wished he felt an ounce of enthusiasm for right now but he didn't, which did not go down with his proud Greek ego very well.

Greek tycoon slain by a Titian-haired witch, he mentally wrote his own tabloid headline. Grimaced then braced his shoulders and went into his office, firmly closing that door behind him too.

Nell came drifting awake to the sound of rattling crockery. It reminded her so much of Thea Sophia that she lay there in smiling contentment, imagining herself to be on the island—until a lazy voice said, 'I hope that smile means you're dreaming about me.'

She opened her eyes to find Xander standing over her, looking lean and mean in his sharp business suit, and reality came crashing in. 'Oh,' she said. 'We're in London, aren't we?'

Yawned and stretched then looked back at him. 'What time is it?'

'Refreshment time,' he said lightly, turning away then turning back again with a tray in his hands.

Nell slithered up the pillows, dragged the sheet up to cover her breasts then yawned again, rubbed her eyes then swept her tumbled hair back from her face.

'Didn't know you did Room Service,' she quipped as a tray arrived across her lap.

'Anything for you, my love,' he responded in the same light vein as he sat down on the bed and removed the cover from a plate of fluffy scrambled eggs piled on a bed of hot toast.

Nell glanced at the half-light seeping through the drawn curtains. 'Is it morning already?' she asked in surprise.

Xander smiled. 'Not quite.' He handed her a glass of freshly squeezed orange juice. 'You've been asleep for hours while I've been chairing the meeting from hell. If the world were flat I would be taking great pleasure in pushing one half of a room of ten off the end of it. Is that OK?' he added questioningly as she sipped at the juice.

Nell nodded. 'Lovely.'

He sent her another smile then forked up some scrambled egg. 'Here, try this and tell me what you think.'

'It's only scrambled eggs,' she derided as she took the forkful into her mouth.

'Yes, but very special scrambled eggs, since they were prepared by my own gifted hands.'

'You?' Nell almost choked. 'I didn't think you knew what an egg looked like in its shell.'

'Shame on you.' He forked up another heap. 'I am very self-proficient when I have to be. Drink some more juice.'

Nell frowned. 'Why did you feel the need to be proficient at this particular moment?'

'Because I decided to leave the ten squabbling in my boardroom and came in here to see you. You were out for the count. I noticed that you must not have woken up to get yourself something to eat and, since you haven't had anything since you threw up on the motorway, I decided that it was time that you did. You can go back to sleep when you've eaten this…'

Another forkful was offered to her. Nell looked at his smooth, lean, totally implacable, super-relaxed face, said nothing and took the fork from him so that she could feed herself. For several minutes neither spoke while Nell ate and he seemed content to watch.

Then it came, the real reason he was sitting there looking at her like that. 'Nell—what I said about your father—'

'Is he still in Australia?'

'Yes,' he frowned. 'You knew he'd committed himself to overseeing the whole project,' he reminded her.

'Yes.' Her sigh was wistful and rather sad.

'I want you to know that I gave you the wrong impression about your father's involvement in our—'

'Oh, I don't think so,' she said as she laid down the fork. 'I think you made your point perfectly. You took me as assurance for your investment. We even have a contract that says so. You also saved me from a fate worse than death.'

A frown pulled his eyebrows together across the bridge of his nose. 'I'll rip the contract up if it will make you feel better.'

'It's so sweet of you to offer,' she mocked him. 'But the gesture would only have some weight behind it if you'd offered to do that *before* I got pregnant.'

'I did offer once before, if you recall.'

'On my birthday?' She looked up at him. 'Before my father had managed to scoop the Australian deal and put his business back on track? Bad timing, Xander,' she said. '*Not* what you're renowned for. You could have been asking to renegotiate yourself right out of the whole deal for all I knew. Still know,' she added when he opened his mouth to deny it.

The fact that he was going to have to pull rabbits out of the proverbial hat to make her believe otherwise now held him silent while he took that on board.

Nell hunted around for something trite to say to fill in the gap.

But what came out was miles away from trite. 'There,' she said. 'Plate cleaned. Baby adequately fed.'

'I did it for you, not the baby!' he snapped.

That she didn't believe him showed. He uttered a sigh, his indulgent manner disappearing without a trace. 'Does it actually matter what motivated me?' he posed curtly. 'Am I not allowed to be concerned for you both?'

He glanced at his watch then and stood up to remove the tray. 'I have a meeting to return to. I'll see you later.'

With that punishing slice of ice, he left. Nell threw herself back against the pillows and wished she knew how she should feel about him, but she didn't. Everything she had come to love and trust about him over the last three weeks had been shattered by a day-long series of hard knocks.

The telephone call from Vanessa being the hardest knock.

Restless now, she got up, feeling an instant chill on her skin because of the difference between a hot Greek summer and a cooler English one. Rubbing at her bare arms, she wandered around the bedroom, aimlessly picking things up, putting them down again, and would have gone and done the same in the sitting room but she couldn't be absolutely sure that someone might not come in from the office and catch her half-naked, and Xander seemed to have forgotten to have her suitcase brought up.

In the end she escaped to the bathroom and decided to indulge in a long, hot soak in the invitingly huge bath. A few carefully placed candles would have been nice to help her relax, but she had to make do with selecting a couple of soft downlighters. She found no sign of any female soapy things hanging around, which mollified her restless mood somewhat.

So Xander didn't indulge his women here, she mused as she lay submerged in hot, steamy water liberally laced with Xander-scented bath oil. Maybe he did have a purple and red velvet-lined pad in Soho. With a mirrored bed and flying cupids embroidered on the velvet, she extended with a soft laugh.

'Cheered up at last?'

'Oh!' She flicked her eyes open to find him casually propping up the doorframe. Sheer surprise had her slithering into a sitting position, causing a minor tidal wave to slosh around the bath. 'You were quick,' she said disconcertedly.

'I didn't like the company,' he drawled, dark eyes glossed by silky eyelashes as he looked her over from loose topknot to water-slicked breasts being caressed by steam.

It was stupid to feel shy after spending three weeks mostly naked around him, but telling herself that did not stop the blush from mounting her skin. Nell tried to make it look casual when she drew her knees up and looped her arms around them. The action did not change that look she knew so well on his lean, dark face.

He'd lost his jacket and his tie, she noticed. His shirt collar was undone and the shirt cuffs too. And if ever a man knew how to lounge sexily in a doorway then Xander had the pose down to a finely tuned art. Long legs relaxed, hands loosely looped in his trouser pockets, silk dark hair finger-ruffled just enough to add that extra brooding appeal.

Her body responded, breasts growing heavy, nipples peaking where she crushed them against her thighs. Even her lips felt as if they were filling and pulsing.

'You forgot my suitcase.' To Nell, it was an inspired stab at the prosaic.

It didn't alter his hungry look one iota. 'Stashed in the sitting room five minutes after we arrived,' he said. 'Didn't you bother to look?'

'No.' She added a grimace. 'Maybe you could get it for me?'

'Why?'

'So I can put something clean on?' she suggested ever so sarcastically to what she thought a stupid question to ask.

Xander clearly didn't. He straightened up and began approaching the bath. 'You can wear me instead,' he murmured huskily and began to undo the rest of the buttons on his shirt.

'Don't you dare try to get in here!' she cried, causing a floor-sloshing wave as she shifted up the bath. 'I'm still angry with you! I don't even like you any more! I will *not* be your sex slave just because you need—'

'Watch it...' His hand darted out, capturing her hair just before it tumbled out of the topknot into the bath.

Shaken by panic, utter confusion and a rotten desire to finish the job with his shirt, she glared at his hair-roughened breastplate while he re-knotted her hair with an infuriating finesse.

'There,' he said. 'Now you won't have to spend half an hour drying it before we get to bed.'

'I'm not sleeping with you ever again.'

'Did I mention sleep?'

Nell tried to calculate if she had enough room to make a run for it while he was busy stripping off his clothes.

'Not a cat in hell's chance,' he teethed out, reading her like an open book.

Stark, blinding, beautiful naked, he stepped into the bath.

'We are not going to let this war continue,' he informed her as he came down on his knees to straddle her. 'You are my wife and you are having my baby.' His hands took possession of her warm, wet, slippery breasts with their tightly distended, lush pink nipples. 'As these beautiful things tell me you want me, *agape*, and as I am so majestically displaying I most certainly want you, why fight it?'

Why indeed? Nell thought helplessly as she, like a captured rabbit, watched him lower his head. It was like being overwhelmed by Poseidon again she likened helplessly as he took charge of her mouth, her body and the rest.

A few minutes later and she was slithering beneath him into the water with her arms clinging to his neck. They'd made love in a bath many times but for some reason this hot and steamy, oil-slicked occasion that was permeated with his scent tapped into another dimension. Water sloshed as they touched and caressed each other, she was so receptive to everything about him that she found she didn't care if her face sank beneath the surface and she drowned like this.

His arms stopped it from happening. The way he was smoothing small, soft, tender kisses over her face kept her breathing slow and deep. His eyes kept capturing hers and filling her with dark liquid promise, when he slipped a hand between her thighs she arched her body in pleasure and captured his mouth.

They kissed long and deep, they moved against each other slowly and sensuously. When with a lithe grace he changed his position, stretching out above her and murmured huskily, 'Open your legs,' she even made the move with a slow erotic invitation that set him trembling as she clasped his face in her hands so she could pull his mouth back to hers as he entered her with a long, smooth, silken thrust.

And the whole thing continued to a slow, deep, pulsing rhythm. His supporting arms stopped her from drowning in the water, while inside she drowned in a different way. When she fell apart she even did this slowly and deeply and the pulses of pleasure just went on and on and on.

When he lifted her out of the bath she clung to him weakly. Even when he dried them both she didn't let go. She was lost, existing in a place without bones or muscles; the only solid thing was him and the thickly pumping beat of his heart beneath her resting cheek.

'If you *ever* let another man see you like this you won't live,' he rasped out suddenly.

Nell just smiled and pressed a silky kiss to his hair-roughened, satin-tight chest. 'Take me to bed,' she breathed.

With a muffled groan Xander lifted her up and carried her into the bedroom, still clinging. She was still clinging when he settled them both in the bed. She fell asleep like that—clinging. Xander lay beside her wondering how long he should wait before he woke her up again.

He used up the time recalling the looks on the faces of the ten men in his boardroom when only half an hour after battle recommenced he'd stood up and brought the whole thing to an abrupt end.

'When you are ready to negotiate like adults let me know. Until then this meeting is over.' He smiled as he saw himself making that announcement because—there he was, being the hard-hitting, cool-headed, totally focused, ruthless dictator. Wouldn't they like to know that beneath the incisive veneer he'd brought that meeting to a close because he'd been aching so badly for this...

His wife. This sensational woman with a silken thigh lying across his legs and her slender arms still looped around his neck. On a sigh because he knew he should not give in yet, he reached up to claim one of her hands then carried it down his body to close it gently around the steel-hard jut of his sex.

'You're insatiable,' she murmured, letting him know that she was already awake.

'For you,' he agreed. She stroked him gently and the whole deep, drugging experience began all over again.

Afterwards he went off to raid the fridge and came back with a bottle of champagne and two glasses, one of which he handed to Nell—already filled.

'What's this?' she demanded, frowning into the glass when it became obvious it wasn't champagne because he was only now easing the cork from the bottle.

'Sparkling water,' he supplied. 'Pregnant women don't drink alcohol.'

'What would you know?' she protested.

About to take a sip at the water, since it was all that was on offer, she found her eyes pinned instead to the way he'd suddenly turned into a concrete block. The lean face, the black eyes—nothing moved.

'What have I said?' she gasped in surprise.

'I just remembered something I needed to do.' He seemed to need to give himself a mental shake before he could bring himself to pour out his champagne. 'Here,' stretching out beside her, he offered his glass up to her lips, 'a sip can't hurt, and a baby is something to celebrate...'

The odd little moment slid by.

Maybe she shouldn't have let it. Maybe Nell should have listened to the little voice inside her head that told her he was hiding something. If she had done then what happened the next morning would not have come as such a crushing blow.

Xander was already in his office and working at his desk by the time Nell sauntered out of the bathroom wrapped in a fluffy white towel. She was aching a little because Xander had been so unquenchable last night. Gentle though, she recalled with a soft smile, unbelievably gentle, as if his knowing about the baby had brought out in him a whole new level of tenderness.

Her inner muscles quivered, her expression taking on a far-away look as she allowed herself the luxury of reliving some of those long, deep, drugging kisses they'd shared, the fine tremor of his body and the look in his dark eyes just before he'd allowed her to take him inside.

If that look didn't speak of love then she'd been dreaming it, she thought as she went over to her suitcase, which Xander had thoughtfully placed open on a low cabinet by the window.

There again it could be just that, having forced herself to accept that since she did not have the power to resist him she might as well stop trying to fight him, maybe she was justifying that by misreading the look.

Oh, shut up, she told that cynical side of her nature. Do you want to spoil it? They were man and wife in every which way you wanted to look at it now that they'd conceived a baby between them, which in turn meant that they were now so deeply committed to this marriage that the Vanessas of this world could take a hike, because no other woman would ever have what Nell now had of Xander.

His first child growing inside her. A child that Xander had spent the rest of the night protecting with the gentle spread of his hand. Did it matter if this had all started out three weeks ago with him determined to achieve that goal?

At least she did not disappoint, she mocked with a grimace. And turned her attention to sifting through the clothes one of the maids on the island had packed for her. One day, she thought ruefully, she might get to pack her own suitcase; then she might find something she wanted to wear.

They'd awoken to a cold, grey day this morning. Even with the temperature in here maintained by an air-conditioning system with climate control, her skin was wearing a distinct chill. The suitcase contained a choice of lightweight short white cotton skirts and a couple of white strapless tops or the turquoise dress.

On a sigh she selected some underwear, dropped the towel and slipped into bra and panties followed by the turquoise dress, then looked around her for something to cover her chilly shoulders and goose-pimpled arms. The suit she had travelled here in lay across the back of a bedside chair but the thought of putting on the travel-limp jacket did not appeal.

On impulse she walked over to the wide walnut-faced wardrobe and opened the doors. Xander's clothes hung in clear plastic from their hangers. Business suits, dinner suits, shirts, ties. Nothing there she could borrow that would keep her warm, she thought ruefully and flipped her search towards the column of deep drawers built into the wardrobe. She found socks, men's undershorts, even a neatly stacked drawer of plain white T-shirts. A foray into the final drawer offered up a better prospect of neatly folded sweaters made out of the finest cashmere. It was probably going to drown her but as she dipped down to near the bottom of the pile to remove a black one she'd spied there, she decided that beggars couldn't be choosers and at least she would be adequately covered.

Then her fingertips came up against the sharp corners of something. On a softly yelped, 'Ouch!' she withdrew her fingers, checked she hadn't managed to draw blood, then frowningly began carefully lifting out the sweaters layer by layer until she'd uncovered the guilty object.

After that she seemed to lose touch with reality. The stack of soft sweaters she held in the crook of her arm fell unnoticed to the floor. She didn't even attempt to pick up the silver-framed photograph she'd uncovered but just stared into Vanessa's beautiful smiling face then at the miniature-sized version of Xander standing laughing in front of her then finally—most painfully—she read the hand-scrawled inscription. 'To Papa Xander,' it said. 'Love from your Alex.'

His son even had his name…

CHAPTER TEN

GLANCING up as Luke Morell stepped into the office carrying a manila file, Xander took one look at his PA's sober expression and sat back in his seat with a smile.

'Did you have to mop blood up off the floor last night after I left?' he quizzed drily.

'You know as well as I do that your shock tactic sent all ten into freefall.'

'Good. Let us hope they learned what it feels like to lose their only parachute.'

Managing a small grimace at the quickness of his employer's wit, 'They want another meeting today,' Luke informed him. 'Perhaps you could try to be a little more—tolerant?'

'For what purpose?' Xander asked. 'I am not into salving other people's egos.' Losing all hint of his own smile, he sat forward again. 'They would not want to meet with me at all if they had done their own jobs better so don't ask me to feel sorry for them. What's with the folder?' he prompted. 'Yet another set of impossible proposals from them?'

'This has nothing to do with the takeover.' Luke walked towards him, his grim expression more keenly in place. 'I suppose I should add that you are not going to like this, so I suggest you take a deep breath before you take a look inside.'

Curiosity piqued, Xander was about to accept the file when a quiet knock sounded at the door through to his private apartment. As he was about to flick his attention from the file to the door he saw Luke stiffen jerkily and his eyes narrowed and remained riveted where they were. He didn't like that telling bit of body language. He didn't like the way his assistant's face had closed up tight. A sudden warning prickle shot across the back of his neck, the kind his instincts had taught him never to ignore.

Then the door-handle began to turn and he was forced to shift his attention to Nell as she stepped into the room. He frowned when he saw that she was wearing the blue suit she had travelled in yesterday, and her hair had been contained in that braid he didn't like. But it was her face that held him. She wasn't smiling, her vulnerably kissable upper lip stuck in a downward curve to its fuller lush partner, and even the light layer of make-up she was wearing could not disguise her odd pallor beneath.

'What's wrong?' he asked instantly, springing to his feet. 'Do you feel ill again?'

He was already striding out from behind his desk as Nell fluttered an unhappy glance at Luke then quickly away again.

'Y-yes—n-no,' she replied in confusion, clearly disconcerted to find Luke Morrell standing there.

'Well, which is it?' Xander demanded, coming to a halt directly in front of her then frowning down at her when she hooked in an unsteady breath of air before focusing her eyes on a point between his tie knot and his chin. 'Nell...?' he prompted huskily when she still didn't speak.

'I'm—fine,' she told him. Then her gaze made another sliding glide towards the very still Luke.

Xander took the hint. With a twist of his long body sent an impatient glance at the other man. 'Later, Luke,' he dismissed him.

Luke hovered, seeming undecided as to whether to walk out with the file or place it on the desk before he left.

'Leave it.' Xander made the decision for him. And after another moment's hesitation, the file was relinquished and Luke was letting himself back out of the room.

'OK.' Xander swung back to Nell the moment they were alone again. 'Now tell me.'

He'd barely got the command out when one of those wretched telephones on his desk started to ring. On an impatient apology he spun away and strode back to the desk, leaving

Nell standing there feeling dazed and dizzy, hating him so much yet hurting badly at the same time.

'Xander—'

He snatched the phone up, cutting short what she had been going to say as he snapped his name into the mouthpiece.

It was like a replay of the day before, Nell thought as she stared at the long, lean length of his dark-suited figure standing in profile against a backcloth of an unrelieved grey English sky.

Beautiful, she observed helplessly, and with an almost masochistic need to feed the ache throbbing inside her began absorbing every elegant inch of him from handmade shoes to the breadth of his wide, muscular shoulders dressed in the best silk tailoring money could buy.

The man with everything, she thought, and had never felt so bitter than she did at that moment. The sensation crawled along her flesh like icy fingers and she knew suddenly that she had to get away—from him, from this raw feeling of utter betrayal, from the sound of his deep velvet voice that was twisting her up inside because she loved that sound even while she hated him.

'I'm going out,' she announced in a breath-shaking whisper and headed jerkily for the outer office door, not caring if he'd heard her, not caring if he would have the usual objections ready to voice at her going anywhere without his say-so.

The telephone crashed with a slam. He moved so fast she'd barely taken two steps before he was catching hold of her wrist and swinging her round. The whole quick manoeuvre brought back memories of the way he'd done the same thing on the island only yesterday.

Her face paled, lips trembling as she released her breath. 'Don't manhandle me.' She yanked her wrist from him.

That he was totally taken aback by the venom in her voice showed in his shock-tautened face. 'What's the *matter* with you?' he bit out.

'I am not some object you can push and tug around as your mood takes you,' she hit back.

He stiffened up. 'I never meant—'

'Yes, you did,' she cut in. 'You think you own me right down to my next thought. Well, you don't.'

'This is crazy,' he breathed in total bewilderment. 'I left a beautiful, warm and contented woman only an hour ago, now the shrew is back.'

Nell deigned not to answer that. She had been warm and contented. She had been nicely, carefully, *patiently* seduced into being that pathetic creature again. She despised herself for that.

'And why are you wearing the same clothes you had on yesterday?'

The sudden flip in subject sent her vision oddly blank as she stared down at the summer-blue suit. It took a really agonised effort to make herself reply without flinging the *why* at him. But she didn't want to tell him. She did not want him to start explaining and excusing his rights over her rights.

'It's all I've got to wear unless you want me to wander around in the turquoise dress,' she said. 'Whoever packed for me at the island packed for the Greek climate, not this one. So I am going out—to shop.'

It was thrown down like a challenge. Xander's dark head went back as he took that challenge right on his cleft chin. He knew what she was saying. He knew which particular gauntlet was being handed out this time. As the tension built and he fought to hold back the instinctive denial that was lodged in his throat, Nell stared fixedly at nothing in particular and hoped to goodness that the fine tremors attacking the inner layers of her skin were not showing on the outside.

'Wait for me,' he said, cleverly couching that denial in a husky dark plea that, in spite of everything, touched a tingling weak spot. 'We will go together. Just give me a couple of hours to free myself up and we can—'

The telephone began to ring. His dark head twisted to send the contraption a look of angry frustration but his fingers twitched by his sides and Nell almost managed a mocking laugh because she knew he was itching to answer that call. His priorities were at war. She twisted back to the door. Behind her she heard Xander hiss out a curse about irritating women.

'Have you any money?' he sighed out then, work winning over his marriage, though to be fair to him he didn't know that—yet.

'I have credit cards.' A dozen of them linked to his accounts.

'Nell…!' he ground out as her hand caught the door-handle. She turned her head to find him already back at the desk with his hand covering the shrilling phone. 'Don't be long,' he husked.

She nodded, lips pressed together to stop them wobbling, then she let herself out of the room. As she braced herself for the walk down the long corridor towards the lift, she said a silent goodbye to him.

Back in his office, Xander was ignoring the ringing phone and snatching up his mobile phone instead. He hit fast dial. 'My wife is just leaving. See that she's protected,' he instructed.

Then he was stepping to the window, hands dug into his pockets, fingers tightly clenched into fists while he grimly waited for Nell to appear on the street below while the telephone continued to ring off its rest.

He did not understand any of that, he decided tightly. He'd thought last night that they'd called a pretty effective truce. Suddenly she was back to sniping at him and evading eye contact. He missed the eye contact. He didn't like the tingling feeling that was attacking the back of his neck.

He saw her step out onto the busy pavement, continued to watch as she paused and looked around as if she had no idea where she wanted to go. His heart gave him a tug, yanking at his gut and contracting it because even from way up here she looked so—lost!

As she seemed to come to a decision and struck out to the left Xander watched Jake Mather slip into step behind her. He remained where he was with his eyes fixed on the top of her shining head until she had disappeared out of sight with her bodyguard safely in tow. Then he turned away from the window and stood grim and tense, feeling unfathomably like a man who'd just made the biggest error of judgement he was ever likely to make.

The phone had finally given up though, he noted, and, straightening his wide shoulders, he stepped up to the desk, hovered on another few seconds of inner restlessness, then the manila file Luke had brought in caught his eye.

Recalling his PA's grim words of warning did not ease the tension singing inside him as he sat down, picked up the file then drew in the advised deep breath.

A breath that froze even as he opened the front flap. A breath that he did not release for the several long minutes it took him to scan the pages set in front of him. By the time he'd finished he felt as cold as death.

She was away for three hours and in that time Xander was in touch with every step that she took. Grim, cold—face stretched taut by the burning pulse of anger he was keeping tamped down inside.

Work had ceased. *Life* had ceased, he mused harshly. Beyond the four walls of his office a series of instructions was being carried out to the letter while he sat in grim isolation, telephones, people, everything shut out but for his mobile link to Jake Mather.

If she bolted she would not get five paces before Jake would have her in his grasp. If she was foolishly letting herself believe that safety lay in the heaving crowds she was trying to lose herself in then she was in for a hard knock of truth. Jake had been joined by his other men, one of which was in the process of tracing the call she had just made from a public call box. Xander had not enquired as to how this could be done. He did not want to know. But behind the cold mask he was wearing on his face he knew that the name Marcel Dubois was about to be quoted at him.

It was.

'Where is she now?' he scythed at Jake Mather.

'To be truthful, boss, I think she's on her way back to you.'

To be truthful, Xander mimicked acidly, he knew that Nell must know by now that she did not have another choice.

She thought he lived in a zoo? Well, now she knew what it felt like, having been swarmed all over by his security people since she'd stepped onto Oxford Street.

Though he now had to accept that he was going to be disappointed that she did not require bundling into the back of the limo that was loitering in a side-street, ready and prepared to receive its protesting package.

Satisfaction coiled around his tense chest muscles when Jake's voice arrived in his ear with, 'Turning into the street now…'

He was out of the chair and swinging to the window before the final word left his security guard's lips. Something hard hit him in the chest as he caught sight of her head with all of its glorious, bright Titian hair shimmering around her face and shoulders instead of being neatly contained in the braid she'd left with.

Xander found himself gritting his teeth as he absorbed her purposeful stride. She was angry. Good, because so was he. If she wanted all-out war he was ready for it.

She was carrying the distinctive yellow and black bags from her wild buying spree in Selfridges. She'd changed her clothes too. The summer-blue suit had gone and in its place tight designer jeans that moulded her long, sensational legs and a soft brown suede jacket that hung loose across a creamy coloured top.

If she'd deliberately chosen the clothes to make him sit up and take notice then she could not have done a better job, because he was seeing her exactly as he had first seen her when she'd walked through her father's front door, wild and windswept. As she turned to walk up the grey marble steps to his building she paused and looked up and, as if she knew he was watching her from up here, her green eyes suddenly sparked and tossed up bolts of burning fire.

'Well, come on up, my fiery witch,' he invited beneath his breath.

Turning, he broke the connection with Jake Mather then reached out to flip a key on his computer keyboard to bring his glass and steel foyer up on to the screen. As he watched his wife stride purposefully across the foyer via the in-house CCTV system he was lifting his jacket from the back of the chair and smoothly shrugging it on. Her barely concealed patience as she rode alone inside the steel-cased lift held his attention while his fingers dealt with his shirt-collar button and straightened his tie. By the time she began the long walk down the corridor towards his office, his finger-ravaged hair had been neatly smoothed and he was ready for her.

Nell pushed open the door and stepped into the room, green eyes flashing like emerald storms. The door slammed back into its housing and she dropped the bags then speared those eyes on Xander, who was casually swinging in his chair behind the desk, looking as crisp and as sharp as he'd looked when she left him—and of course he was holding a telephone to his ear.

Her fury hit boiling point. 'Would you like to explain to me where the heck you get the stone-cold arrogance to believe that you own my life?' she shrilled.

Without so much as a flicker in response from those long dark eyelashes, he murmured some very sexy Italian into the phone's mouthpiece, then gently replaced it on its rest.

'If you have a yen to argue the finer points of ownership then by all means do so,' he invited. 'But before you begin you will explain to me please why you needed to spend thirty minutes in the ladies' room in Selfridges. Were you feeling ill again?'

Oh, so casually asked. Nell felt a sudden trickle of ice run right down her spine. 'How many men did you have following me?' she gasped.

'Seven,' he supplied. 'Including Jake Mather, whom I presume you spotted quite quickly—mainly because he was not instructed to hide,' he seemed compelled to add.

'He tried to stop me using a public telephone,' she said tightly.

With the calmness of a coiled snake, he reached out and

picked up the phone then offered it to her. 'Try this one. All calls are free.'

The green eyes sent him a withering look. 'Don't be so obnoxious,' she condemned. 'You have no right to have me tagged, tailed and guarded like some—'

'Animal in a zoo?' he suggested when words failed her. 'Or, more appropriately in this case,' he then added thinly, 'like an untrustworthy wife!'

'*I* can't be trusted?' Nell launched back at him. 'That's rich coming from the most twisted and devious—*Machiavellian* swine it was ever my misfortune to meet!'

'Oh, you met a worse one, *cara*,' Xander drawled.

'What's that supposed to mean?'

Without any warning he lost his relaxed posture to shoot to his feet. 'You were leaving me for him—again!'

With the backcloth of grey Nell could not see his face but she could feel the anger bouncing off him.

'On the first opportunity you were presented with you rang *him*!' he all but snarled.

'You traced that call?' she gasped out in disbelief.

'You make me sick,' Xander announced, then gave a contemptuous flick of a long-fingered hand when Nell just gaped. 'I don't even want to look at you.'

On that damning indictment he swung away to the window, leaving Nell standing there shaking and quivering—not with hurt but in disbelief!

'How dare you speak like that to me?' she shook out furiously.

'Easily.' Twisting back, he picked up a manila file from his desk, brandished it at her then dropped it again. 'The police report on your accident,' he incised. 'You may read it if you wish.'

But Nell did not wish. Nell was already striding across the office and pushing open the doors to his apartment.

'You were not driving that car!' he flung after her. 'The angle of your seat belt burns proves it! You were sitting in the left seat, not the right—and if I drove myself more frequently in England I would have realised that as soon as I clapped eyes on your bruises and you would have been dead!'

Her face white, her lips clamped together in a flat line of disgust that was ripping her apart inside, without a pause in her stride she threw open the next set of doors, aware that Xander was tracking right behind her. Aware that in one small, satisfied way she had taken him by surprise by walking away.

'You are so in love with the guy that you told nobody that salient fact!' he rasped out from the bedroom doorway. 'You have been protecting him from taking any blame even though the lily-livered coward slunk away from the scene, leaving you lying there badly injured and in need of help!'

All the time he was tossing his accusations at her Nell was throwing the doors open wide on his wardrobe and dragging open his sweater drawer. The soft cashmere garments landed in a discarded scatter. If Xander had been in a more sensible state of mind he might have been forewarned as to what was about to hit him.

As it was he strode forward, gripping the manila file as if it was some kind of weapon. Now she spun on him and it was so *nice* to watch his breathing still when he saw the expression of icy distaste on her face.

'He did not slink away. I sent him away,' she corrected. 'As you say, I protected him from you and your lynch mob and what you might do to him.'

'Because you love him.' He sounded hoarse.

Nell nodded. Why deny it? 'In the same way you have been protecting your family—because you love them?'

The sarcastic tilt in her questioning tone floated right by him. 'You are my family,' he ground out.

'No—here is your family, Xander,' Nell said quietly, and placed the framed photograph down on the bed. 'Goodness knows why you didn't marry Vanessa and give her and that— little boy who looks like he loves you very m-much the right to use your name.' She sucked in a dreadful, choked breath. 'But don't ever dare refer to me as your family again because

I'm not—they are. I think it's time that you got your priorities right and owned up to that.'

He seemed to be having difficulty taking it all in. Nell stared up at his blank, taut face and waited for some kind of response. But all she did see was his eyes shifting from her white face to the sweaters scattered on the floor before slowly, almost unseeingly moving to the bed. As understanding did begin to dawn she watched his face slowly leech of its rich golden colour then his eyes turned black.

'I can explain this—'

'No.' Nell shook her head. 'Explain to *them* why you dared to marry *me*!'

'But this is crazy!' He suddenly exploded back to life again. 'I *can* explain this—!' he insisted.

'But I don't want to hear!' she all but screamed at him.

His eyes flashing black with rage now, he stepped round the bed, slamming the manila file down as he came towards her. The file landed right on top of the framed photograph, Nell saw in dismay.

'You did that on purpose,' she shook out accusingly.

He didn't even bother to deny it. 'I would love to know,' he gritted, 'how you've managed to turn this into a fight about them instead of one about your bloody lover!'

'I h-hate you for that.' Nell wasn't listening. 'How could you do that to that poor little boy?'

Taking hold of her shoulders, he gave them a small shake then pulled her hard up against his chest. 'Listen to me when I speak,' he ground out. 'They are not important. You—your Frenchman is!'

'He isn't French, he's Canadian,' Nell mumbled, still staring at the way he'd covered the photograph as if he'd committed some mortal sin. 'He's also my—'

'Canadian...' Xander repeated as if a whole load of pennies had just dropped into place. 'You stupid fool, Pascalis,' he growled furiously at himself. Then those expressive black eyes flared Nell a look of blistering contempt. 'What did the two of you do—make love on a mountain while your mother lay dying in her bed—?'

The crack of her hand landing against the side of his face made a whiplashing echo around the room. Nell stood locked within his iron-hard grip, panting, breasts heaving as she watched her finger marks rise on his cheek. There was a horrible moment while she stared into those black eyes when she thought he was going to retaliate.

Then he let go, his fingers unclipping from her shoulders before he took a step back. The moment he did Nell began to shiver. Pale as death now and still shocked by her own act of violence, a cold chill shook her, bringing her arms up to hug her body, tense fingers clutching at the soft suede sleeves of her jacket.

She took in a slow breath. 'As I was about to say before you said w-what you said, Marcel is not my—'

'Well, I know he did not taste the main treat, *yenika*,' he drawled insolently. 'But there is more to sex than a—'

'He's my *brother*, you filthy-minded beast!' Nell flung at him.

It was as if someone had plugged him into an electric socket, the whole of his posture racked up with a jerk. '*Theos*,' he husked. 'That was a joke—yes?' Then as he stared into her angry face, '*Theos*,' he breathed again. 'You are serious.'

'H-half-brother,' she extended in a trembling voice.

Violently, he twisted his back to her, lifted up a long-fingered hand and grabbed the back of his neck. Blistering tension was scored into every bone and sinew.

'You should have told me.'

'Why?' Nell quavered.

'*Why…?*' He swung round to spear her with a piercing glare. 'I did not know you even had a brother! Don't you think such a thing warranted a mention some time in the last year?'

'If you'd cared enough about me to want to *know* about me you would have found it out!' she shrilled. 'And anyway…' she pulled in a deep breath '…I enjoyed watching you squirm. It made a pleasant change from squirming myself.'

'What is that supposed to mean?' he demanded stiffly.

Nell felt the sudden threat of wounded tears. 'I was in love with you when you asked me to marry you. I don't think you even noticed or cared!'

'I cared,' he grunted.

'So much that you were with your mistress a week before you married me! Now I find out that she has your child!'

White-faced now, 'No,' he said. 'Listen to me…' He took a step towards her, one hand reaching out, but Nell backed away.

'I w-was going to leave you today.' She shook out the confession. 'If it hadn't been for your men dogging my every step I would have disappeared and you would not have found me.'

The way his jawline gave a tense twitch made her wonder if he was biting back the desire to argue with her about that.

'You play with people, Xander. You like to be in control and when you're not you react as if we have no right to pull on your strings! I've seen you do it with your mother. You did it with those ten men last night. You're *always* doing it with me. You did it today when you set your hounds on me—'

'You said it yourself you were going to disappear—'

'That was my choice!' she launched at him, felt the tears start to come and had to tug her fingers up to cover her quivering mouth. At the same time her other hand went to her stomach because it was beginning to feel strange, kind of achy and quivery and anxious.

'Nell…'

One hand covering her mouth, the other her stomach, Nell was already spinning away. She made a dash for the bathroom with no idea that Xander was right behind her, so he took the full force of the door slamming shut in his face.

CHAPTER ELEVEN

FOR a few blinded seconds Xander just stood there with that solid wall of wood a mere hair's breadth from his face and the whole of his front vibrating from the force with which the door had shut.

Still reeling from the stuff that Nell had thrown at him, he spun to face the other way.

Her half-brother.

'Hell,' he muttered thickly.

His eyes went to the bed and the manila file and he went over there and snatched it up with some deep-ridden desire to toss that damn thing across the room—only he saw the photo frame he'd uncovered and he froze as he stared down at the lovely smiling Vanessa and a laughing Alex.

'To Papa Xander, love from your Alex', he read and the oddest kind of laugh broke from his throat.

Then the sound of retching filtered out through the bathroom door and he was dropping the file again to stride back the way he had come. Even as he pushed open the bathroom door and saw her hanging over the toilet bowl guilt was dealing him a well-deserved punch to his gut because he had allowed himself to forget her delicate condition while they'd been fighting like cat and dog.

Nell heard him arrive just as she was shuddering into stillness. 'Go away,' she whimpered, only to discover that talking was enough to set the whole thing off again.

Two seconds later he was taking control of the situation with the same grim, silent efficiency he had used on the motorway the day before. When eventually it was over and she'd rinsed her mouth out with a mouthwash, he lifted her limp, wasted and hot body into his arms and she discovered she had no strength left to fight him off.

'I hate you,' she whispered instead.

'*Ne,*' he agreed, carrying her into the bedroom.

'I wish you'd never set eyes on me.'

'*Ne,*' he agreed again, reaching down to toss back the covers before bringing her gently down on the edge of the bed.

'My feeling like this is your fault.'

'Entirely,' he admitted. 'Relax your arms from my neck so I can remove your jacket...'

It was the most humiliating part of it all to realise how she was clinging to him. Her arms dropped heavily to her sides. He removed the jacket while she watched his totally expressionless face. No man should be that good-looking, she thought bitterly. It gave him unfair advantage in the jaws of a fight because she wanted so desperately to reach out and kiss him that she felt dizzy all over again.

Her new flat shoes came next, landing with a clunk on the floor. His sensual mouth set straight, eyes hooded by those glossy black eyelashes, he then laid her back against the pillows with extreme care before shifting down her body to unzip her new jeans; a second later and the denim was sliding off her legs with a deft expertise. As the cool air hit her clammy flesh she began to shiver and, with his lips now pinched back against his set teeth, he covered her with the duvet then stepped back and proceeded to yank off his jacket followed by his tie.

'Don't you dare!' she gasped in quivering horror.

'Don't be stupid,' he growled back. 'I might be a control freak but I am not a sadist.'

The next thing his shoes had been heeled off and he was stretching out beside her and tugging both Nell and the duvet into his arms. She curled herself right into him then burst into tears. It was like throwing open a floodgate; she just couldn't control it. With the top of her head pressed into his chest she sobbed her heart out while he lay there and held her and said absolutely nothing.

It was as if every hurtful thing he'd ever done to her came

out for an airing in those tears. The way he'd made her fall in love with him then asked her to marry him in that cool, grim tone she only noticed much later when it was too late. The way he'd stood over her while she signed his rotten pre-nuptial without batting an eyelid because she loved him and trusted him then discovered the painful way that love *was* blind! If Marcel hadn't emailed her urgently with a link to the gossip pages of an American tabloid, she would have sailed down the church aisle to him in a besotted haze.

'I h-had to marry you,' she sobbed into his shirt front, unaware that he hadn't been in on her first wave of grievances. 'I was scared you'd pull out of the deal with my father.'

'Shh,' he said, tangling his fingers in her hair and pressing her closer.

'I f-felt like a child-bride in a regency m-melodrama—s-sold to the unprincipled rake then dropped like a hot potato w-when he got more than he bargained f-for.'

She'd spent the next year pining for what might have been and wishing she'd stayed blind.

'Marcel wanted to come and get me then but I wouldn't let him. I *played* the child-bride in a regency melodrama, h-hoping you were going to turn up one day and realise you were head over heels in love with me but you didn't.'

'You saw me as a self-obsessed rat and I probably was then but you were so innocent and naïve you didn't have a clue what was happening around you. I was trying to protect you until you—'

'Enter the hero stage left,' she mocked thickly, rolling away from him and reaching out for the box of tissues that sat on the table by the bed. Fingers trembling, she plucked a tissue free and sniffed into it. 'Right in the knick of time he saves the innocent twit of a girl from the ugly guy with the f-fat lips.'

There was a shimmer of movement behind her that made her twist sharply to look at him. But if he was laughing at her it wasn't showing on his face. The tears clogged in her throat because it wasn't fair that he should have such liquid, dark,

serious eyes that seemed to be trying to tug her right inside him.

'Nothing to say?' she challenged.

'I will not answer these charges while you're so distressed,'
he said flatly, then on a sigh when fresh tears welled he moved
to pull her back to him again. 'Tell me about your half-brother,'
he prompted huskily.

'He's the son my father wanted from my mother but never
got.'

'So he's younger than you?'

She nodded. 'Nineteen. My mother was already pregnant
with him when she left us. He lives with his father in Banff.'

'You were miserable being married to me. You needed a
shoulder to cry on so you rang him up.'

'Someone I knew loved me.' She gave another nod, thereby
missing Xander's infinitesimal wince. 'I didn't expect him to
climb on the next plane to England to come and sort you out.
He had no idea who he was dealing with. It was almost a relief
when Hugo Vance refused him access to the house.'

'Why did he do that? If he's your brother of course he's
welcome in our home!'

'Marcel wasn't on your very short accepted list.' Nell sat up
and used the crumpled tissue to dab her eyes again. 'And he
might only be nineteen but looks a lot older because he's big—
six feet three already and built to suit—a heck of a sportsman;
can white-water raft like you would not believe.'

'You're proud of him.'

'Mmm.' It was that simple and neat. 'I think Hugo Vance
felt threatened by him.'

'How is it that you or your father have never so much as
spoken his name to me?'

'My father refuses to have his name mentioned because he
blames Marcel for stealing his wife away. He's still hurting.
I've just got used to never mentioning him because that's the
way it's always been. And anyway, you and I didn't have the
kind of relationship that encouraged sharing secrets.'

A small silence followed while Nell dabbed at her eyes and

Xander lost himself in deep thought. Then he hissed out a sigh. 'The irony of it,' he muttered.

Nell didn't find anything ironical in what had been said.

'Why was he driving your car?' he asked suddenly.

She gave a small shift with her hunched shoulders. 'Because I let him,' seemed excuse enough because the hell if she was going to admit that once she'd escaped Rosemere she then had a stupid change of heart and got so upset about it, Marcel had to drive because she wasn't fit to.

'OK…' said with such slow patience Nell knew that he knew she was fobbing him off. 'Explain to me, then, if he's so into playing your hero, why he ran away from the accident scene.'

'He didn't—and don't you *dare* speak of Marcel in that nasty tone!' She swung on him angrily.

'Now I know why I'm jealous,' Xander said bluntly.

Nell looked away again, refusing point blank to take up that comment. 'He wasn't licensed to drive here,' she admitted grudgingly. 'He wasn't used to our narrow, winding lanes,' and he wasn't used to driving such a small but very powerful car. 'When he lost control on the bend I thought we were both going to die…'

A hand arrived at the base of her spine, long fingers rubbing in a strangely painful, comforting stroke. 'But you didn't…' he said gruffly.

Nell shook her head. 'Marcel wasn't wearing his seat belt.' It was just another thing she'd felt guilty about. She'd been so stupidly upset she hadn't noticed he hadn't belted himself in. 'If you want irony,' she mumbled, 'when he was thrown out of the car he suffered barely a scratch.' She grimaced into the tissue. 'When I realised how bad things were for me I was scared for him. I convinced him to lift me into the driver's seat then begged him to leave. He wouldn't go. He was upset, angry with himself, scared for me—and I've never seen him look so young and helpless…' The hand at her spine rubbed again, she quivered on a sigh and swallowed fresh tears. 'He used my mobile phone to call an ambulance then stayed beside me until we heard it arrive then he hid in the woods until I was safely inside the ambulance. I was so worried about him, I got a nurse in A&E to call his mobile and reassure him I was absolutely fine.'

'I didn't know that.'

'Don't sound so surprised,' Nell flung out. 'You might be the control freak around here but I know how to get my own way when I need to. I picked a young student nurse with her romantic ideals still intact. She thought she was calling up my lover—she adored being a part of my wicked tryst.'

'You amaze me sometimes,' he laughed though it wasn't really a laugh. 'I truly believed you were the most open and honest person I know but you can lie with the best of them!'

Her shrug told him she couldn't care less what he thought or believed.

'Where was he staying?' he bit out next. 'I had every hotel and pub for miles around carefully combed for him without getting back a single damn clue!'

'He was backpacking. He camped out in a farmer's field.'

'Enterprising of him.'

'He's very self-sufficient.'

'Matinée-idol material.' His hand left her back.

He really was jealous. Nell smiled into the now crumpled tissue. Then he uttered another one of those sighs and tried to pull her back down to him but Nell refused to go.

'I want to go to Rosemere,' she announced.

'I want you here with me.'

Just like that, quietly spoken but deadly serious. Nell turned to look at him and found those jet-glossed eyes roaming over her with blatant messages.

It wasn't fair. She looked away again as a whole gamut of weak sensations went sweeping through her. 'I'll stay married to you until the baby comes.'

'Thank you,' he said.

'But afterwards we get a divorce.'

'You need another tissue, *agape mou*. That one is just about done.'

'I'm being serious!'

'So am I. You are about to start weeping again and that tissue has mopped up too many tears as it is.'

And those tears just returned all the harder. 'I can't seem to switch them off,' she sobbed.

'Come here.' This time he refused to take no for an answer so she landed in the crook of his arm. 'You are just in need of some tender loving care right now.'

'Not from you.'

'Yes, from me. Who else have you got?'

It was so brutally frank that she winced.

'Tell me why the call you made to Marcel today was traced to Paris.'

'He's been staying with the French side of his family. I knew he was flying back to Banff today so I wanted to catch him and doubly reassure him that I was OK before he left.'

'Was he reassured?'

Nell nodded but kept her mouth clamped tightly shut as to how she had given that reassurance.

'I would like to have listened in on that call,' Xander drawled with lazy amusement.

He knew, the beast. He knew she'd convinced Marcel that she was gloriously, happily in love with her husband.

'I thought you had meetings to attend,' she prompted.

'I am attending to you.'

'Well, I can—'

'Remain right where you are.' Tightening the hold he had on her, he rose up until he had her pinned to the bed. 'I am the control freak,' he murmured huskily. 'Be controlled or watch me get upset.'

Green eyes searched gently mocking dark ones. He was gorgeous—irresistible. He kissed her—lightly on both corners of her vulnerable mouth, on the warm, soft, tear-swollen bottom lip then tracked a whole line of soft kisses along her jaw until he reached that sensitive spot by her ear. Things she did not want to happen started to happen. Nell quivered out a sigh of discontent. He caught it, tasted it with his tongue and she felt the blunt jut of his desire thicken against her thigh.

'No,' she said. 'I don't want—'

To do this, she was going to say but the moment she opened her mouth to speak the gentle dart of his tongue stole the rest away. With the arrival of his fingers across her cheekbones he deepened that kiss, making love to her mouth with a slow tenderness that had her shifting restlessly beneath his weight. Each time he paused he looked deep into the conflict taking place in her eyes, if she tried to say anything he returned to the kiss until eventually she forgot what it was she wanted to protest about. Her fingers shifted, relaxing out of the tense fists she had them clenched in to begin a slow foray across the leanness of his taut hips to his waist and eventually with a slow, shuddering sigh over warm flesh covered by cool white shirting to his shoulders, his neck and with a final convulsive move buried them in his hair.

She was lost, his for the taking. The duvet was pushed aside. The only time he allowed her to think was those few too brief seconds he required to remove the rest of her clothes and even then the moment she showed signs of protesting he was back again, smothering out everything but him and what he was doing and how he was making her feel.

His own clothes disappeared by degrees, she didn't even notice until the manoeuvre was over and she was being overwhelmed by the fully naked male. He made love to her breasts, so acutely receptive that she stretched into a lithe, sensual arch, toes and fingers curling in drowning pleasure that earned her yet another deep kiss to her mouth. And he was trembling, she liked that. Her restless hands crowded each muscular flex and quiver until, 'Touch me,' he groaned and she did, closing her fingers around smooth silk on steel and felt him throb and thicken then lost touch with her breathing when his long fingers tested the wetness between her thighs.

Bright rainbows of colour began to dance on her senses, and he answered them with a thick, hoarse growl. His heart was pounding, hers was pounding, as he eased his weight between her spread thighs then made that smooth drive into her, and she opened her eyes to look at his harsh look of hungry passion etched on his face.

'I don't want to love you this badly,' she confided on a sad little whisper.

He lost control. She'd never known him do it so thoroughly before so the difference between smooth, slick, sophisticated lover and a man lost in the wild, throbbing beat of his desire was startling. All she could do was hang on for dear life as he drove the two of them to the edge then over it in a wild, hot charge that threw him into a paroxysm of gasps and shudders that just seemed to go on and on.

Afterwards, exhausted, she thought she might have actually lost consciousness. She certainly didn't remember another thing until she awoke much later to find herself alone in the bed with the cringe-making knowledge that once again she had allowed him to whittle away at what bit of pride she had left by letting him make love to her.

And not only make love—which was bad enough—but she'd also let him twist her into such knots by getting her to confess her crimes to him while he got away without confessing a thing about his mistress and his son!

His son. The tears began to sting. Throwing herself onto her back, she stared fiercely at the ceiling in an effort to stem the threatening flood. How could she let him do this to her? How could she *go on* letting him do this to her? She had to get away from him, she knew that now, because she couldn't fight this sexual empowerment he had over her and each time she gave in to it she lost a bit more of herself.

She brought an arm up with the intention of covering her stupid watery eyes—but as she moved the backs of her fingers touched something and, turning, she saw a folded slip of paper lying on the empty pillow beside her head. With her heart lodged in her aching throat, she lifted the piece of paper up then lay there just staring at it.

She was afraid to read it. Really scared because he had never done anything like this before and all she could think was it had to have something to do with Vanessa and that little boy.

Mouth—fingers trembling, she made herself open it out.

'I love you', it said. That was all, nothing fancy, no hearts and flowers, or trumpeting fanfares, just those three words scrawled in bold black pen.

She curled into a tight ball beneath the duvet and cried her eyes out with the note pressed against her breasts.

Getting showered and dressed was an effort. She throbbed and ached and trembled too much to be efficient at anything. Back in the jeans and the cream top and her hair brushed, she pushed open the bedroom door with the intention of going to the kitchen and making herself a fortifying drink before she had to face him again—but it wasn't to be.

One of the doors through to his office had been left spread wide open and the first thing to hit her was the sound of Xander's voice tearing into someone in cut-throat Italian. As her feet drew her unwillingly towards that open door the next thing to hit her was Xander himself wearing one of his dark business suits and looking as razor-sharp as the sound of his voice.

The sun had come out since she'd last seen him standing behind his desk like this, and sunrays were playing across his jet silk hair and the deep bronze sheen of his skin. Angry as he was, he looked magnificent, all-powerful, all-masculine, all hard, dark lines of lean musculature. Animal, sexual, so utterly magnetic that her breathing feathered in her chest and brought her feet to a halt as a wave of helpless, hopeless love swept through her on a shimmering wave of anguished defeat.

Why him? she asked herself painfully. Why did I have to fall for a man like him? Why did he have to leave a note on her pillow spelling out words he had never once said to her face? Guilt? Remorse? Damage control? She couldn't believe those words. How could she believe them when Vanessa and that poor little boy stood in the way?

She went to turn, needing to slip out of sight before he saw her because she just wasn't ready to face him, but as she went to move another voice spoke angrily and her heart sank.

She'd thought he was talking on the telephone. He was *al-*

ways on the telephone! Maybe she uttered the strained little laugh she could feel clogging up her throat because Xander's dark head whipped round.

'Nell…' the hard, husky rasp of his voice scored a shudder right down her spine as still she tried to escape from this.

'No, don't go…' He was already striding round the desk while she hovered reluctantly, several feet into the sitting room. The sound of his swift footsteps sounded in her head then his hand caught her arm just above her elbow. He tried to turn her but when she dug in her heels he stepped around her and reached for her other arm, holding her still in front of him. She could feel his tension, the hot simmer of his anger as his harsh breath scoured the top of her head.

'Look at me,' he husked.

But there was no way she was going to look at him. She stared at the knot in his silk tie instead.

His fingers flexed then began to slide upwards, they reached her shoulders and used them to tug her closer, then moved on to bury themselves in her hair at the defensive curve of her nape. It only took the light stroke of his thumbs beneath her chin to have it lifting.

Once again her breathing feathered as she found herself flickering a dancing glance over his face. Tension packed it, strain, the simmering anger glinting in his eyes. As she fluttered her eyes downwards again she was suddenly caught by the difference in his mouth. Held tight though it was, the fuller bottom lip still protruded more than it should. It looked darker—swollen; a hot tug deep inside her abdomen reminded her how urgently she'd sucked and bitten that swollen bottom lip—clung to it in the wild throes of—

A tense hiss of air left his throat. 'I know what you're thinking but I don't want you to think,' he said fiercely. 'I want you to stay calm and for both our sakes trust me, *agape mou*. I can explain myself—'

'With little notes left on pillows?' It was out before she could stop it.

'Little notes left on pillows can be read and reread,' he

pointed out. 'If I said those words out loud they would be swallowed up by too many conflicts rattling around in your head right now.'

Well, he was oh, so right about that. 'I can't do this any more,' she told his shirt front. 'You play games with me, Xander. You make me feel like your stooge.'

'You are not the stooge around here, *cara*. I am—someone else's stooge. But it is going to stop.' It sounded more like a threat than a promise. 'All I need from you is your patience. I *can* explain this.'

'Will you stop saying that? And don't you dare kiss me!' she protested when he started to lower his head. 'You think you can just kiss away every objection I put up against you but you can't. I—'

'If you two are going to start that again I may as well leave you to it…'

As if in a daze, Nell looked around, saw her mother-in-law—dressed goddess-style in wine-red silk—appear in view. She blinked, stunned that she could have so easily forgotten that Gabriela was even there! Then she became aware of other things, like the way she and Xander were standing in the doorway, almost wedged there by his rock-solid, unyielding stance. Her hands were on his chest, palms flat, fingers splayed. His still curved her slender neck. But worst of all her hips were resting against his hips. They didn't need to be pressing that close to him but they were as if they couldn't help themselves.

A rush of colour burned into her cheeks. As if he knew why it did, Xander slid his hands down her tense back to her hips and crushed her even closer, then did what she'd told him not to do and kissed her on the mouth.

'Don't so much as move another foot near that door, Madre,' he murmured with cool threat as he lifted his head again. 'It is judgement day, and you will not get out of this building until you have paid your dues to my wife.'

Judgement day? Pay her dues? Nell stared up at him with a mind gone blank.

He ignored the look, and suddenly he was all sharp and businesslike again. 'In here, I think.'

Looping an arm around Nell's shoulders, he turned her into the apartment then led her over to a chair then pressed her down into it.

'Don't tremble so much,' he scolded quietly.

'I...'

He kissed her fiercely—again.

'Oh, stop it, *caro*,' his mother snapped out impatiently as she appeared on the threshold of the apartment. 'Can't you keep your hands off her for five minutes? Helen is not going anywhere, as apparently I am not. *Dio*, Helen,' she added with a small shiver. 'How can you stay in this soulless place? I always hated it. Demitri never managed to get me to stay here once.'

'Did he ever get you to do anything you didn't want to do?' her son shot back at her.

'Oh, that's so unfair!' Gabriela protested. 'And so typical of you, Alexander, to always take your father's side!'

'You made him miserable—'

'I made him happy!' his mother angrily declared. 'How dare you, with your own marriage hanging in the balance by what I choose to reveal here, stand there and judge mine?'

They were suddenly back to fighting across the width of the sitting room, and doing it in English this time so Nell could at least understand the words if not the reasons for them. Looking from one face to the other, she couldn't decide which of them was going to catch light first. Xander was a proud Greek by birth but a hot-tempered Italian by nature, and she wondered if he had a clue as to how much like his mother he was?

'I can judge because I had to live with it.'

'Poor little rich boy, so badly treated,' his mother mocked. 'Helen, what is that top you are wearing?' Gabriela turned her attention away from her angry son to toss some derision her daughter-in-law's way instead.

'Leave Nell out of this,' her son hissed as Nell cringed into the chair feeling like a rag doll suddenly.

'I think she's already very much *in* it.'

The fact that her dry point hit home showed in the way Xander stiffened his elegant shoulders.

'Maybe you're right.' He took in a deep breath, then next thing Nell knew he had moved to stand behind her chair and his hands were settling on her shoulders in a possessive act no one could mistake. 'Congratulate us, Madre,' he then murmured dulcetly. 'Nell and I are going to have a baby, which means that you are going to be a grandmother...'

CHAPTER TWELVE

GABRIELA went so white that Nell thought she was going to faint on them and tried to rise to her feet to go to her.

'Remain where you are.' Xander's hands kept her seated. 'She will recover in a moment.'

'How can you be so heartless?' she gasped.

'I find it remarkably easy,' he answered coolly.

'But she's in shock—'

Gabriela gave a slow—slow blink of her beautiful eyes.

'I am all right.' Her pale mouth even managed to stretch into a wry little smile though her usual grace was missing as she walked to the nearest chair and slowly, carefully sat herself down. 'A *bambino*…' she whispered dazedly. 'Now, that, *mia caro*, was quite a blow even from you,' she admitted.

'As you can tell, my mother is not very enamoured with babies, *agape mou*,' Xander drawled lethally to Nell.

'It is not the *bambino* part that repels me but the *nonna* part,' Gabriela inserted surprisingly. 'Now I understand your desire to have me explain about Vanessa and her—son.'

Nell immediately began to stiffen. 'The desire for you to explain has always been there.' Xander's hands tightened on her shoulders in a gentle but determined squeeze. 'You simply chose to ignore it.'

'Until now…'

'Until now,' he agreed. 'So start talking or so help me, Madre, I will publicly denounce you as my mother and acknowledge them!'

Nell was beginning to feel sick, very sick. A hand went up to press against her mouth. Gabriela saw it and a look of what could have been remorse crossed her beautiful face.

'Our apologies, Helen,' she sighed. 'You have no idea what

169

we are talking about and therefore are thinking the very worst. Alexander, Helen needs a glass of water,' she concluded quietly.

With a soft curse he took his hands from her shoulders, his angry steps took him into the kitchen then seconds later brought him back again, then the man himself appeared in Nell's vision, squatting down in front of her to offer her a glass of cool water at the same time that he touched a concerned hand to her warm brow then was lifting her fingers from her mouth and carrying them to his lips.

'Sorry,' he said gruffly. 'This was not supposed to turn into a battle in front of you. I hoped that you would sleep a little longer so we could get this part out of the way before you needed to hear.'

'Hear what?' Nell tugged her hand free. 'That you have another family out there that is more important to you than your own mother—or me, come to that?'

'That just is not true.'

'You know about Vanessa and the boy?' Gabriela murmured in surprise.

Stupid fresh tears sprang into Nell's eyes as she sipped at the water. Robbed of her hand, Xander brought his to rest against one of her pale cheeks.

'Start talking, Madre,' he rasped out.

Gabriela flinched at the serrated edge to his voice. 'I had an affair with a man half my age,' she confessed in a reluctant rush.

'And broke my father's heart—'

'He broke mine too! Vanessa is only a few years older than Helen! He should have been shot for taking such a child to his bed!'

Vanessa? Nell's attention picked up. She glanced at Xander to find his gaze fixed on her, narrowed and intent.

'Both you and your father had an affair with Vanessa?' she breathed in stricken horror.

Anger reshaped his mouth. 'No, we did not,' he denied and

sprang up and spun away, angry tension racked across his shoulders.

Gabriela sighed. 'You are such a fool, Alexander,' she informed him. 'Have you never learned how to get your priorities right?'

'Like my father did?' he lashed back.

'*Sì!*' Gabriela cried. 'As we both did!' she impressed. 'You cannot pick between the two of us when you look for faults, Alexander. It just is not fair!'

'You took another lover before he did,' her son dismissed that line of defence.

'And he had his revenge.' Gabriela took in a deep breath and returned her attention to Nell. 'You cannot begin to know about middle age until you reach it, Helen. No one can—not even the great Alexander, who apparently has never put a foot wrong in his life!'

As a dig at his marriage to Nell, it hit the mark.

'Middle age eats away at your heart and your belief in yourself. You see lines where only smoothness had once been and a sagging figure where once everything had been tight. You see younger women receiving the admiring looks you used to receive.'

'You break my heart.'

'Be quiet!' his mother responded. 'You're a man,' she said in disgust. 'You do not fade like an ageing rose, you improve year by year! Your father did this! He improved and improved in his physical stature *and* he admired these younger women while assuring me I looked *nice*. Have you any conception at all how badly *nice* can hurt?' She swung on Nell again. 'If my son ever uses that word on you, *cara*, then take my lead and find yourself another man, preferably one a lot younger than he is—'

'You're careering from the point,' Xander incised.

'Feeling the vulnerability of your age difference to Helen's, *caro*?' Gabriela incised back. 'When you hit your fifties she will still be in her thirties—the absolute prime of a woman's life!'

'Get to the point!' The tension in him was close to snapping. Nell blinked at the sight of darkness scoring the rigid line of his cheeks.

'At least you chose the child for your wife, not your mistress,' his mother continued with the same cutting scorn. 'I am the same age as your father. I *felt* it deeply when his interest began to stray. You are built in his image—a true Pascalis male who will not lose his good looks and his sex appeal as he grows older.'

'So you jumped on the first man that showed you some admiration.'

'I did not jump, I *dived*,' his mother declared without conscience. 'I lost myself completely in the glorious flood!'

'You have no shame.'

Nell stood up. 'I think I should leave you two to finish this on your—'

'Sit down again!' Xander thundered.

Her chin came up. 'Don't speak to me like that.'

With a flare of rage he stepped up to her and forcibly made her sit. She'd never seen him like this, so controlled by his emotions that he was almost fizzing. She opened her mouth to protest. He covered it—hard. Yet even though it began as an angry way to subdue her, the kiss did not conclude that way and she could feel the effort it took for him to drag his mouth from hers.

'Listen to what she has yet to say—please,' he begged, and when she could only nod, he claimed her mouth again, soft with gratitude—then moved away.

Having watched the little interplay with interest, oddly, Gabriela went quite pale. 'My son loves you—'

'The point, Madre,' Xander curtly prompted.

'He made me come here because he said you would not believe a word he says about this—thing with Vanessa DeFriess.'

'Liars lose the right to be believed,' Xander inserted.

'I still don't understand why you felt you needed to lie!' his mother cried. 'What man with a beautiful wife to love would want to lay claim to that—*puttana*? Unless, of course, you were... Ah,' she said when he all but threw himself over to the window.

'Stop trying to outguess me and spit it out,' Xander gritted.

'Well, he was lying.' She turned back to Nell again, and then took in a deep breath. 'It was *my* husband who had the affair with Vanessa,' she spelled it out at last. 'Demitri took that woman to his bed to get his revenge on me. When the madness was over for both of us and we decided we could not live without each other, we made a promise that neither affair would ever be spoken about again.' She paused to take in a breath. 'All was well for several months. Indeed, we enjoyed the bliss of a second honeymoon.' Her beautiful dark eyes took on a wistful glaze. 'Then Vanessa came to Demitri and told him she was pregnant with his child. Everything fell apart in that moment. After Alexander was born and I discovered I was unable have more children Demitri had assured me that it did not matter...'

'I didn't know that,' Xander murmured gruffly.

'No.' His mother looked at him. 'You believed I was a fashion plate with a thin figure to protect. And you are now thinking of your own lonely childhood when I was not a very good mother to the one child I did have,' she tagged on to his hard expression. 'Which I suppose does give you every right to look upon me with such cynicism. I *admit* that I am not the maternal kind.'

It was like listening to some bizarre rehash of her and Marcel's story, Nell thought as she listened, while her mind stung her with disbelief. Coincidences like this just didn't happen. It was reality gone berserk. She looked up at Xander to find his fierce gaze was fixed on her.

'I know,' he said tensely, reading what she was thinking. 'This is why I knew you would not believe me if I told you this myself.'

His mother looked from one to the other. 'What are you talking about?' She frowned.

'Nothing,' Xander said. 'Please continue.'

'Continue.' Gabriela laughed stiffly. 'What is there left to say? There was your father, about to become a father again and he could not disguise his delight. I was going to lose him again and I was so terrified I—took an overdose and had to be flown to hospital. By the time I was out of danger Demitri was a different man. I begged him to never see Vanessa and her baby and, to his word, they were never mentioned again.'

'How much more proof could he offer that he loved you?' her son put in. 'He handed responsibility for Vanessa and his unborn child to me with the instruction that I never speak of them because he would not have you distressed like that again.'

'And you never forgave me for being so spineless.'

'The child has rights,' Xander said. 'You gave him none. The mother had the right to be treated with respect if nothing else. You denied her that right. She was gagged so quickly by my father's lawyers that she was left without a single leg to stand upon.'

'For money,' Gabriela pointed out. 'Don't forget the millions you take care of for her. Or the huge trust set up in the boy's name.'

'Or the hours of emotional support both Vanessa and her son required once Alex was born. I became a father without taking part in the act of conception and I do not recall you ever feeling sorry for my plight.'

'You didn't have to take duty to such extremes—'

'He's my half-brother!' Xander expelled in hoarse-voiced fury. 'Half my own flesh and blood!'

'I know I am a very selfish woman,' his mother said shakenly. 'I know you see me as a spoiled, vain, useless waste of space. But it is happening again, isn't it?' She looked helpless suddenly. 'You are willing to sacrifice me for them just as your father was willing to do the same thing.'

'No,' Xander uttered gruffly.

'You already threatened it, Alexander,' she wearily reminded him. 'Your father did the same.'

'Hence the dramatic overdose aimed to pull him back into line again?' Xander said hardly. 'If that isn't extreme then I don't know what is, Madre. Now I've made you talk about this, am I to wait with bated breath for you to use the same emotional blackmail on me?'

His mother went white. On a gasp of horror at his cruelty Nell shot to her feet. 'Xan—'

But Gabriela got in first. 'I have my regrets, Alexander,' she told him stiffly. 'And I can now feel the cutting pangs of remorse for denying your father the right to know his other son. But if you believe I have not been punished very adequately for my sins then you're wrong. When Demitri died I lost a major part of myself. I still miss him so much...'

'You know,' Xander drawled, 'I would respond kindly to that blatant attempt to play on my sympathies if it was not for the fact that only minutes before Nell came in you were still refusing to sacrifice your ego for the sake of our marriage.'

Gabriela accepted this final indictment with a wry little smile. 'Ah, that sin called ego,' she drily mocked herself then turned to go.

'No—don't go,' Nell begged huskily. 'You both need to resolve this...'

Gabriela looked into her daughter-in-law's anxious face then at Xander's rock-like stance and offered up a grimace. 'You are a sweet person, Helen. You will make a good mother to my grandchild. Let us hope that my son will be a good father, for I think he forgets that I was not the only parent to leave him for another love.'

Then she walked away, leaving Nell staring helplessly after her while Xander continued to stand there like a cold, hard, *stubborn* fool!

'Go after her.' She swung on him urgently. 'She's your mother, for goodness' sake. You love her, you know you do— faults and sins alike!' When he still didn't move from his stiff stance, 'If you let her go now you will never see her again because the *both* of you are too stuffed full of pride to give a solitary inch! I thought you were bigger than this! Xander, please...!' she begged painfully.

But she didn't need to add the last part because with a tight, angry growl of blistering frustration he spun and strode after her, leaving Nell staring after him feeling very much as if she'd just been run over by a pair of trucks.

She watched his hands reach out to grasp Gabriela's narrow shoulders, watched through a deepening glaze of tears as he turned her into his chest. She caught the tones of thick, gruff, husky Italian, felt her heart quiver as the proud Gabriela broke her control on a muffled sob.

Then she turned away and began to shake like a leaf, still too befuddled by what she had been told to even attempt to sort it out in her head.

She made for the kitchen, leaving mother and son alone to mend their differences while she attempted to do something really normal like setting about making coffee but feeling so at odds with herself and with Xander that she didn't hear him arrive at the door.

'OK?' The husky question came from behind her.

Stiffening her spine, she pressed her lips together and nodded, not sure she wanted to look at him until she'd made up her mind if she hated him for putting his mother through that ordeal, or loved him for doing it for her.

'No more nausea?' he questioned when it became clear she wasn't going to speak.

'I'm fine,' she managed, fingers fiddling with the slender white china cup she'd set out ready for her coffee. 'Would you like a drink?'

'Not if you're planning to poison it,' he said drily, then hissed out a weary sigh. 'Nell, we need to—'

'Your telephone's ringing.'

And it was. They both listened to it for a few fraught seconds, Nell with her eyes squeezed tightly shut on a tense prayer that he would just go and answer the damn thing. Xander, she was sure because she could feel it, piercing the vulnerable tilt of her neck with grim intent in his gaze, wanted her to turn and look at him.

'Easy on the belladonna,' he instructed heavily after a moment and went back to his office, leaving her wilting though she didn't really know why.

A few minutes later she was bracing her shoulders and carrying two cups of freshly made coffee into his office. Xander was still on the phone with his dark head resting back against the chair's leather upholstery, and his eyes were closed. He looked tired, she noticed, dragged down and fed up. As she walked across the expanse of floor towards the desk she saw his lashes give a flicker and quickly looked away.

'*Efharisto,*' he murmured as she put one of the cups of coffee down in front of him.

She managed a brief upward glance at his face before turning away again.

'Stay,' he husked, showering her in tingling tremors. 'Sit down, relax, drink your coffee. I will be only a few more moments here.'

Sit down, relax, drink your coffee, Nell repeated silently and sank into the chair by his desk and wondered why she was still feeling so at odds with him when everything had been explained—hadn't it?

He was talking in Greek, she noticed, sitting up now and swinging his chair slightly with his eyes lowered to where a set of long fingers hit intermittently at the computer keyboard lying on the desk. His deep voice was quiet, asking low key questions with no hint of sharp command evident, as if someone had switched off his normal incisiveness.

The phone went quietly back on its rest. Strumming silence followed. Nell felt it so deeply inside that she tensed.

He picked up his coffee cup and looked down into it. 'How much belladonna?'

'Two spoonfuls,' she answered.

'Still not forgiven, then.' He grimaced a wry smile at her then lifted the cup to his lips and drank. The way that he did it was so much like a man willing to take his poison that she shot like a bullet to her feet.

'Stop it,' she stabbed at him.

'Stop what?' He looked at her.

'Making a joke of it.'

'Of what?'

'All of that—stuff we've got through today.'

'Are we through it?'

She frowned at the question, her tightening nerve-ends forcing her to discard her coffee-cup before she spilled it down herself. 'Y-your mother is your mother.'

'Is that supposed to make some sense to me?'

'Sh-she is what she is and you have to accept that.'

'I do—as much as I can do,' he reminded her. 'Next problem.'

The way he said it as if she was in a business meeting made her start to seethe. She jerked round to face the other way. 'I don't like you.' That was a problem, she thought. 'Sometimes…' she then added grudgingly because it was crazy to deny that she liked him in bed—*loved* him in bed.

Loved him all the time, she extended unhappily, but loving didn't have anything to do with liking, did it?

'You hurt people and don't seem to care when you're doing it.'

'Are we still discussing my mother?'

'No—me,' she said huskily.

Silence met that announcement. Nell folded her arms beneath her breasts and stared down at her feet.

'You should have told me the truth about Vanessa.'

'You should have told me the truth about Marcel.'

'That was different.'

'Why?'

'Because he wasn't an issue when you married me. Vanessa was and once you knew it you should have told me the truth straight away instead of letting me spend the next twelve months imagining you in her arms instead of mine!'

A sigh sounded behind her. The next sound was the creaking of his chair as he came to his feet. Her chin hit her chest when he came to stand right in front of her. Without saying a word he clamped his hands to her waist and lifted her up to sit on the desk. Next her thighs were summarily pushed apart and he was wedging himself between them, then her arms were firmly unfolded and lifted round his neck.

'OK,' he said. 'Now that we are more comfortable I will explain... I fell in love with you within about two seconds of you walking through your father's front door...'

Her chin shot up, green eyes wide with shock and disbelief.

'Got your full attention now?' he mocked. 'Ready to hang on my every word with bated breath?'

'You never did love me then, or you would not have left me on our wedding night believing what I did.'

'You are referring to that memorable time when you stood there in your bridal gown, shouting at me and looking so heart-breakingly beautiful, hurt and *young*?' He uttered a sigh. 'It was either leave you there or toss you on the bed and ravish you and—trust me, *agape*—you would not have survived the kind of ravishing I had in mind right then. I was mad with you for believing that trash—mad with myself for not seeing it coming. Do you think that Vanessa is the only skeleton a man like me has lurking in his closet? I've had women trying to foist their babies on to me and women trying to blackmail me. I've had them sneaking into my bed in the dead of night and crawling through windows in an effort to get to me.'

'Oh, don't be modest; do tell the rest,' Nell drawled acidly.

'You think I like being every greedy gold-digger's dream catch? Why do you think my security is so tight? Would you like a ballpark figure on how much it has cost me to keep such stories out of the Press over the years? Give any one of those grasping women a glimpse at more money and they would be singing to the Press today. Vanessa was the exception. She was not my skeleton, which made those computer printouts you showered at me all the more annoying because I did not feel I had the right to break the promise of silence and protection I had made to my father on his death bed.'

'Not even to me?'

'Don't look so hurt,' he chided. 'Do you think it didn't hurt me to realise that you were not equipped with the necessary defences to live my life? I already knew I'd been unforgivably selfish, crowding you into marriage so young. I saw in a single miserable flash of enlightenment as I watched you enact that little tragedy just how selfish I had been. I saw how every jealous woman out there was going to have a story to whisper in your ear. It would have been like leading a lamb into a slaughterhouse then standing back to watch it be skinned.'

'So you walked away.' Her soft mouth wobbled.

'Yes.' He kissed the wobble then sighed. 'When I left you at Rosemere I did it determined to set you free—but I could not. I kept on putting it off. Kept coming to see you, couldn't stay away! Kept trying to convince myself that while you seemed content with what you had then you were OK. The night I offered to renegotiate our contract was the one time I was ready to rip the damn thing up and let you go. I've never felt happier when you turned the offer down without even hearing me out. I was off the hook for another few months until my conscience got to me again. Then that second photo of me with Vanessa appeared and you crashed your car. I've never felt so bloody lousy in my entire life!'

'Good,' she said. 'It's nice to know that I wasn't the only one feeling like that.'

'Ah, but that was before I knew about the new man in your life.' He smiled. 'I switched from feeling lousy with remorse to a thirty-four-year-old lusty, cradle-snatching lecher in a single blink of an eye. You think you were jealous of Vanessa? You barely scratched the surface of jealousy, *agape mou*. But I did. I scratched it right down to its bloody, primitive raw.'

'I love it when you're primitive.' She moved a little closer in an effort to capture his mouth.

His head went back. 'I'm being serious!'

'So what do you want me to say—get away from me, you uncivilised beast? Shall I get your pack of bodyguards to string you up to a tree and tar and feather you for wanting me too much to let me go?'

'Loving you too much,' he corrected softly.

'And aren't you the lucky one that I loved you too much to drive away…?'

'What's that supposed to mean?' He frowned at her.

Nell gave a little idle shrug. 'Only that Marcel was driving me *back* to Rosemere when we crashed. I thought your police report would have told you that.'

'If it did, I never got to read that far,' he murmured dazedly. 'I just read the bit about you being in the passenger seat and went berserk.'

'I noticed,' she murmured feelingly.

'Forgive me for what I said?'

Nell shook her head.

Xander uttered a sigh then changed tactics. He lifted her up until she straddled him then strode across the room.

'Where are we going?' she asked innocently.

'Guess,' he drawled. 'If I am to pay a penance then I will do it in comfort.'

And he did.

The island was trapped in the sultry heat of the late afternoon when the helicopters began to arrive. From her place at the nursery window Nell watched as Marcel jumped down onto the ground then walked towards the glinting pool. He looked so absolutely gorgeous that Nell uttered a small sigh of sisterly pride. A sudden cry of delight went up, then a young boy in swimming shorts was racing to meet him. Marcel grinned lazily as he accepted this show of pure hero worship from the much younger Alex.

'My hero status has been eclipsed by the matinée idol,' Xander murmured with a regretful sigh.

'Never mind, your real son worships you,' Nell consoled. 'And look at your mother and my father watching them together. They're actually smiling. That has to be a first for both of them.'

'It's called bowing to fate,' Xander said. 'They either accept our family as a whole or they miss out.'

'And who'd have thought Gabriela would be so besotted?'

'Why should she not,' Gabriela's son defended loyally, 'when my son looks exactly like me?'

'Too like you,' Nell complained, turning away from the window to go and lean over the cot, where Demitri Pascalis lay kicking contentedly. 'Now, you know I love you,' she informed the wide-eyed baby. 'But I still don't think it's fair that you didn't even elect to have my green eyes.'

The baby let out a shriek of delighted laughter. He didn't care that he looked the absolute spit of his dark-eyed *papa*.

'Cruel,' she scolded. 'But I will get my own back,' she warned him.

'And how do you intend to do that?' Xander asked.

Straightening up to find herself slipping easily beneath his waiting arm, Nell smiled one of those wait-and-see threats at him as she let him lead her away.

'I see,' Xander murmured fatalistically. 'The wicked witch is mixing spells again.'

As they left the baby's room Thea Sophia slipped quietly into it, and took the comfortable chair placed by the cot. Out came her lacework and her gnarled fingers got busy while the baby chatted away to her. He would fall asleep in a few minutes, bailing out with a blink of an eye, but until that happened he had his ever-attentive *thea* to entertain.

Walking Nell into their sunny bedroom, Xander turned her to face him. He was dressed in one of his loose white shirts and casual trousers, but soon they would have to start getting dressed up for the party that was to take place tonight—which was a shame, in Nell's opinion, because she preferred to keep him in clothes she could strip off quickly.

'Mmm,' she said as she pressed her lips to the triangle of hair-roughened flesh exposed by the open neck of his shirt. 'You taste of sun and salt and sexy masculinity.'

'And you have a one-track mind,' he sighed.

'It's my birthday. I'm allowed a treat.'

'Several treats.'

'OK,' she shrugged, not arguing the point because it was oh, so much more interesting to discover how smoothly the shirt fell open to her lightest touch. She ran her fingernails down his front and watched taut muscles flex.

'You're so gorgeous,' she murmured helplessly—and received her reward with the hungry clamp of his mouth.

It didn't take much longer for them to be lost. Xander's muttered, 'We don't have time for this,' was ruined by the urgency with which he stripped her blue T-shirt dress off her and tumbled her onto the bed. They made hot, frenzied love while the rest of the family chatted by the poolside.

When they came downstairs two hours later you would be forgiven for thinking that Nell had spent the whole afternoon achieving that gloriously chic look she'd donned in a short half-hour. She was wearing aquamarine silk, smooth and slinky, a perfect set of blue diamonds sparkling at her creamy throat.

Her hair was up to show them off because Xander had given her them for her birthday. And if anyone wondered at the rueful grimace he offered when his mother congratulated his wife on how two hours' pampering could put such a wonderful glow to her daughter-in-law, no one would have thought to question whether he knew something that they did not. He looked far too smooth and sophisticated to be recalling what they'd been doing in the shower only half an hour ago.

They separated, they danced and circulated amongst their fifty-strong guests as goods hosts did. They laughed and teased and flirted and came together on the terrace to snatch a private moment or two gazing at the moon.

'Happy?' Xander asked, holding her in front of him.

'Mmm,' Nell murmured uncertainly.

'Something missing from your perfect day?'

'Mmm,' she nodded.

'You would like me to toss you into the pool perhaps?'

'Not tonight, thank you,' she answered primly, then took hold of one of his hands and slid it over her abdomen. 'I'm afraid it's tender loving care time again,' she softly confided.

Xander immediately stiffened like a man in shock. 'I hope you are teasing me!' he grated.

'No,' Nell sighed.

He swung her around, a dark glitter in his eyes. 'You mean you really are pregnant? But our son is only ten months old!'

'I want a red-haired, green-eyed girl child this time,' she told him. 'And you really are lousy at birth control.'

'Ah, so I am to get the blame again.'

'Of course,' she said then wound her arms around his neck and leaned provocatively into him. 'But then you never, ever disappoint…'

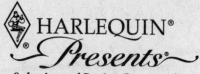

eHARLEQUIN.com

The Ultimate Destination for Women's Fiction

Visit eHarlequin.com's Bookstore today for today's most popular books at great prices.

- An extensive selection of romance books by top authors!

- Choose our convenient "bill me" option. No credit card required.

- New releases, Themed Collections and hard-to-find backlist.

- A sneak peek at upcoming books.

- Check out book excerpts, book summaries and Reader Recommendations from other members and post your own too.

- Find out what everybody's reading in Bestsellers.

- Save BIG with everyday discounts and exclusive online offers!

- Our Category Legend will help you select reading that's exactly right for you!

- Visit our Bargain Outlet often for huge savings and special offers!

- Sweepstakes offers. Enter for your chance to win special prizes, autographed books and more.

Your purchases are 100% guaranteed—so shop online at www.eHarlequin.com today!

If you enjoyed what you just read,
then we've got an offer you can't resist!

Take 2 bestselling love stories FREE!
Plus get a FREE surprise gift!

This June

Silhouette®

⌐SPECIAL EDITION™¬

Presents the exciting finale
of the continuity

MONTANA MAVERICKS

GOLD RUSH GROOMS

Lucky in love—and striking it rich—
beneath the big skies of Montana!

MILLION-DOLLAR MAKEOVER
by Cheryl St.John

In the ultimate rags-to-riches story, plain-Jane Lisa Martin
learns that she's inherited the Queen of Hearts gold mine.
Yet the idea of being rich and powerful is foreign to the
quiet, bookish young woman. So when handsome
Riley Douglas offers to join her payroll and manage the
property, Lisa is grateful. But is Riley too good to be true?

Available in June 2005 at your favorite retail outlet.

Silhouette®

Where love comes alive™

Introducing a brand-new trilogy by

Sharon Kendrick

**Passion, power and privilege—the dynasty
continues with these handsome princes…**

THE ROYAL HOUSE OF CACCIATORE

Welcome to Mardivino—a beautiful and
wealthy Mediterranean island principality,
with a prestigious and glamorous royal family.
There are three Cacciatore princes—Nicolo,
Guido and the eldest, the heir, Gianferro.

This month (May 2005) you can meet Nico in
THE MEDITERRANEAN
PRINCE'S PASSION #2466

Next month (June 2005) read Guido's story in
THE PRINCE'S LOVE-CHILD #2472

Coming in July: Gianferro's story in
THE FUTURE KING'S BRIDE #2478

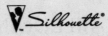

SPECIAL EDITION™

Discover why readers love Sherryl Woods!

THE ROSE COTTAGE SISTERS

Love and laughter surprise them at their childhood haven.

For the Love of Pete

by

SHERRYL WOODS

Jo D'Angelo's sisters knew what she needed—a retreat to Rose Cottage to grieve her broken engagement. And their plan was working—until Jo came face-to-face with the first man ever to break her heart, Pete Catlett, who had ended their idyllic summer love affair when he got another girl pregnant. Pete vowed to gain Jo's forgiveness for his betrayal...and perhaps win her back in the process.

**Silhouette Special Edition #1687
On sale June 2005!**

Where love comes alive™